The Measure of More

We Were Created for More
But Not More of the Same

Bryan M. Williams

THE MEASURE OF MORE

We Were Created for More—
But Not More of the Same

Bryan M. Williams

STERLING
LOGIA PRESS

Contents

Introduction

We live in a world that measures relentlessly —measuring achievement, productivity, success, status, and influence. From the moment we wake, we are invited into a current of "more": more to do, more to earn, more to prove, more to become. But beneath the surface of that striving, a quieter question lingers: *What kind of "more" actually matters?*

This collection was born from that question.

The Measure of More is not a single narrative, but a mosaic of lives—people who, in ordinary moments, confront the dissonance between the life they're chasing and the life that might actually lead to wholeness. Some of these characters are driven professionals; others are aging dreamers, uncertain teens, or weary caregivers. All of them are wrestling, in their own way, with the gap between what the world celebrates and what the soul requires.

The stories unfold in a small town much like any other, where front porches sag with memory and silence carries more than sound. As paths cross and choices ripple outward, a thematic thread emerges: being more is often quieter, riskier, and far more courageous than simply having more.

The spiritual undercurrent of these stories owes much to thinkers like Dallas Willard, whose work quietly shaped the questions behind these pages. His call to resist hurry, to pursue formation over performance, and to live from the center of a well-anchored soul runs just beneath the surface here. This is not a collection about religion, but about grace—how it breaks in, disrupts, and gently reorients lives toward something deeper.

You won't find sweeping climaxes or grand declarations in these pages. Instead, you'll find doorways—small, human-sized thresholds where characters pause, turn, or stumble into something that asks more of them and, at the same time, offers something better.

Because we were created for more—but not more of the same.

Thank you for walking alongside them. And perhaps, in these reflections, you'll hear echoes of your own journey—measuring not just what fills your calendar or resume, but what fills your heart.

— *Bryan M. Williams*

Dedication

For Wendy—

You live with integrity, walk with honesty, and inspire me without trying. These stories carry your influence in more ways than you know.

Author's Note on AI Use

Some passages in *The Measure of More* were drafted or refined with the assistance of artificial-intelligence tools. In my process, AI functioned much like a human assistant—offering prompts, suggesting alternate phrasings, and helping me explore structural ideas. Beyond drafting, AI also supported post-creation tasks such as conducting developmental edits, performing meticulous proofreading, and running consistency checks; these are the very roles that developmental editors, proofreaders, and style managers have long performed in traditional publishing. Throughout the process, every sentence, character moment, and emotional beat was then personally reviewed, edited, and curated to ensure consistency of voice, intent, and craft.

I share this not to distance myself from the work, but to be transparent about my methods —and to affirm that AI, at its best, simply extends the writer's toolbox. Just as authors have long embraced typewriters, word-processors, and thesauri, I believe we can leverage AI responsibly: freeing our creative energy for vision, nuance, and the human truths that machines cannot originate. May this collection stand as proof that technology, when guided by human intention, enriches rather than replaces the art of storytelling.

The Note She Held

*C*allie slipped in through the side entrance. The familiar scent of lemon polish and old hymnals was a prelude to the peace that choir practice always brought her. Today, that peace would shatter quickly.

Afternoon light spilled through stained glass, casting jewel-toned patterns across the empty pews. She exchanged quick waves with Samantha and Amber, her friends from school, and hurried past the other choir members to her usual spot.

"I'm getting excited," Ms. Jenner said, opening a piece of sheet music at the piano. "The concert is nearly upon us. Let's warm up, everyone."

Callie pulled out her phone and pressed the record button.

The familiar notes of "Be Thou My Vision" washed across the sanctuary. Callie joined in softly, finding her place within the tapestry of sound. She could sing with the sopranos but preferred to sing alto adding the counterpoint that, for her, brought depth to the music.

As the second verse began, she felt the song coming from deeper within; the notes rising without effort. She imagined Grandpa Walter's gentle baritone, the way it used to sound beside her in the third pew from the front. The memory wrapped around her like an embrace.

The final notes of the hymn faded into silence. Callie stood anchored in that perfect moment of belonging.

Ms. Jenner stood. "Beautiful work, everyone." She adjusted her glasses and consulted her folder of sheet music and reminders. "Before we continue, I have a quick announcement—Mrs. Anderson, who was going to handle the solo on Easter morning, is out with bronchitis."

A ripple of whispers moved through the choir.

"But no worries—" Ms. Jenner's gaze drifted toward Callie, a small smile forming. "Callie's mom let me know that Callie is ready to step up and handle the solo."

Callie felt as if the sanctuary had suddenly tilted. Her fingers froze mid-fidget on her music folder. Heat rushed to her face as most of the choir turned in her direction.

What? Mom did what? Without asking? The joy of blending in, of being one voice among many, evaporated in an instant.

From the front row, Samantha offered a thumbs-up. Mr. Winters, one of the tenors, nodded approvingly.

"Easter solo," someone whispered. "That's huge."

Ms. Jenner looked directly at Callie, her expression warm. "You're going to do great. Thanks for stepping up."

Callie's fingers found the silver cross at her neck, twisting it once, twice.

"Uh … yeah," she managed, the word barely audible even to herself. She attempted a smile that felt more like a grimace.

The choir director moved on to announcements about rehearsal times, but Callie barely heard. Her thoughts scattered like startled birds. Had Mom really volunteered her without asking? Of course she would.

The choir moved on to their next piece, a more complicated arrangement of "In Christ Alone." Ms. Jenner's fingers danced across the keys, and the altos began their entrance. Callie missed her cue, coming in a beat late. She could feel her face flush and her heartbeat raise further. Struggling, she found her place in the music.

Each note felt mechanical now. She heard herself singing—the slight vibrato, the way her voice curved around certain vowels—as if listening to a stranger. The harmony that had embraced her minutes ago now felt like a spotlight, exposing every imperfection.

She sang the right notes, hit the right rhythms, but the music had become just another task to complete correctly. Another expectation … another duty.

Mom probably told everyone already. Grandpa will want pictures. What if I mess up in front of the whole Easter congregation?

Practice continued around her. The sanctuary's colored light shifted as clouds passed outside, dimming the stained glass patterns.

◆ ◆ ◆

When Callie pushed open the front door, the scent of cooking onions and garlic greeted her. Music played softly from the kitchen radio—one of mom's upbeat playlists. Callie hesitated in the hallway before forcing herself forward.

Her mom stood at the counter, knife moving in quick, precise chops through bell peppers. A half-folded basket of laundry sat beside the kitchen table, forgotten mid-task.

Callie set her folder on the table, the sound catching her mother's attention.

"There you are!" Mom glanced over her shoulder, knife still working. "Congrats, future star! I told Ms. Jenner you'd be perfect."

The words landed like stones. Callie's throat tightened. It was true, then. Not a misunderstanding. Mom had volunteered her. Without asking. Without warning.

Callie stared at the floor. *She really doesn't get it*, she thought. What she said aloud was: "Why didn't you ask me first?"

Mom's knife paused mid-chop. She turned, eyebrows raised as if Callie had asked if water was wet. "Honey, I knew you wouldn't volunteer —you'd never put yourself out there like that." She resumed her rhythmic cutting. "You'd have talked yourself out of it before giving it any consideration."

Callie's fingers tightened around her necklace chain. "But it should be my choice."

"Your voice deserves to be heard. It's beautiful." Mom scraped the peppers into the sizzling pan. "It's a golden opportunity, and you're ready—even if you don't see it."

Callie's reply dissolved in her mouth, unnecessary because Mom had already decided what she should say, what she should want ... what she should feel.

"This could open so many doors for you, Callie. We should record you—get some clips and start building some social media buzz." She paced the small kitchen, energy radiating from her like heat. "I still know people from my college days. Brian Winters teaches at Eastman now. He owes me a favor."

The knife lay forgotten on the cutting board as Mom's hands animated her growing vision. "With your range, scholarships are practically guaranteed. Your grandfather's connections in the legislature could help too."

Callie gripped the counter edge. Each

suggestion made it worse. *Please, just be quiet.*

"We could look at summer intensives, too," Mom continued, speaking faster now, almost breathless. "Get you positioned before senior year even starts."

Callie steadied herself, fingers sliding from the counter. "Mom, it's not just about the solo. Singing —it's ... it's part of me. It's personal. It's kinda sacred. I don't sing for the spotlight. For me, singing is something I give, not something I need to sell."

Mom's expression softened, but only for a moment. She crossed the kitchen and placed both hands on Callie's shoulders, squeezing with what felt like encouragement but landed as just more pressure.

"You're just nervous. Everyone gets stage fright. But you can't hide forever, honey." Her thumbs rubbed small circles, as if massaging away resistance.

Callie stepped back, breaking the contact. "It's not fear. I just don't want to sing for the wrong reasons."

The words lingered in the charged silence between them. Mom's forehead creased, her hand frozen mid-gesture.

"And what does that even mean?" Mom's voice sharpened around the edges. The kitchen light reflected the confusion in her eyes—genuine bewilderment.

"I—" Callie's voice wavered. Would her mom

ever understand that singing for applause felt like betraying something holy inside her?

Words failed Callie as she stood there, unable to bridge the gap between her mother's ambition and her own truth. The tension hung between them, thick and unresolved.

"Let's finish dinner," Mom finally said, turning back to the stove. "We can talk about song choices later."

The conversation shifted to the school week ahead—safer territory. Conflict put away for now, they ate, cleaned up, and settled into their evening routine. Callie took over washing dishes while Mom packed leftovers, the kitchen radio filling their silence with easy melodies.

As water ran over plates, Callie began to hum along quietly to a hymn her grandfather had taught her. The simple act restored some balance inside her. She closed her eyes, finding comfort in the melody's familiar shape. The hum transformed into soft song.

When she opened her eyes, she noticed Mom several feet away, phone raised, recording.

"Just a little clip to show how natural you are. No big announcement or anything," Mom said.

The song died in Callie's throat. She turned off the faucet, staring at the phone capturing her private moment.

"Please don't post that." She dried her hands on a nearby towel.

Mom's fingers were already tapping the screen.

"It's just to get a little buzz going."

She didn't pause at all, but clicked "upload" with casual finality. The intimate moment—Callie's quiet communion with music —transformed into content for strangers' consumption.

Without another word, Callie hung the dish towel and walked out of the kitchen, leaving her mother alone with the soft electronic ping confirming the upload was complete.

Her knuckles barely made a sound as Callie knocked softly on the half-open door. She peeked into the warm glow of the room.

"Hey, kiddo, I didn't expect to see you today." Grandpa's face brightened, the deep lines around his eyes crinkling with genuine pleasure. He waved her in with a gentle sweep of his hand, setting aside the book he'd been reading. "Come in, come in."

Classical music drifted from the television creating a bubble of calm that felt worlds away from the tension at home. Black-and-white photographs watched from the dresser, familiar faces frozen in time.

Walter nodded to the other armchair. "Sit down, tell me everything that's going on in the big wide world out there." After a moment's fumbling, he managed to click off the television.

Callie pulled off her jacket in the too-warm room, and settled into the chair. The familiar scent of grandpa's aftershave was like aromatherapy. "We're preparing for the Easter musical. The music is amazing. I brought you a sample." She scrolled through the recordings on her phone, finding the one she'd made during rehearsal. Her thumb hovered over the play button for a moment before pressing.

The melody filled the small room. Her voice, slightly louder than she would have liked, joined with the rest of the choir as the Easter hymn rose and fell.

Walter folded his weathered hands neatly in his lap. A smile spread across his face by the second phrase, not the false, discerning smile of a judge, but one born of joy and peace. He swayed slightly, almost imperceptibly, with the cadence.

When the final note faded, Walter said, "You sound just like your grandmother did when—"

"Beautiful work, everyone," the recording continued. "Before we continue, I have a quick announcement—"

Callie quickly stopped the playback.

Walter's gaze lingered on the now-silent phone. "You look rattled. What's going on?"

Callie hadn't intended to bring this up, but she honestly felt that Grampa Walt might be the only person who would understand how she really felt.

"It's a mess." The confession slipped out. "Mrs. Anderson is sick, and mom nominated me for the solo in the concert. I just want to sing with the choir ... I don't want the spotlight. It seems like everyone, especially mom, wants it to be ... bigger. Brighter. Louder." Her hands lifted in a helpless gesture, trying to encompass everything —her mother's videos and ambitions, the constant push toward visibility and exposure.

Walter tapped his cane twice against the floor, a habit that preceded his most honest thoughts. "Sounds like some people, your mother included, want a show. Feels like you want to just enjoy being a part of something real. That's not the same thing, and sometimes, it's like water and oil."

Grandpa hadn't dismissed her concerns or told her to be grateful for the opportunity. He'd simply recognized the truth. Callie felt that he, at least, was on her side.

A light knock interrupted their moment— three quick taps in a rhythm that could have been the start of a song. Meredith Jacobs appeared in the doorway, a wide grin spreading across her face beneath perfectly applied red lipstick and carefully styled white hair.

"I thought I heard a familiar voice in here ... one that I've heard recently on the internet! You're going places, kid." Merry bustled into the room without waiting for an invitation, her floral scarf trailing behind her. She beamed at Callie. "That tone—pure as a bell! Just needs a little polish and the right push." Her rings flashed as she gestured enthusiastically. "I've got contacts from my cruise ship days. People who know people."

Walter smiled politely, his hands resting on his cane. He offered no comment, just a slight nod.

Callie's smile thinned. Her fingers twisted together in her lap, picking at a loose thread on her sleeve.

"Your grandpa must be proud. Raising a star." Merry chuckled, swaying slightly as she spoke, oblivious to the tension she'd brought into the room.

The warmth that had enveloped Callie moments ago cooled into discomfort.

Merry twirled her ring, already halfway into a monologue about stage presence. "You know, I could show you a few tricks—projection, posture. Essential for making an impact."

Walter caught Callie's eye and tapped his watch. "Merry, forgive me, but I've got my medication schedule."

"Oh! Of course, of course." Merry patted Walter's shoulder. "We'll talk soon, Callie. That voice just needs the right showcase!"

After her clicking heels faded down the hallway, Walter shook his head with gentle amusement. "What she called a showcase ... that's not what your heart is asking for."

The quiet that returned to the room felt sacred again. Callie exhaled, releasing the tension she hadn't realized she was holding in her shoulders.

"I knew you'd understand." She glanced at the hymnal on his shelf, its worn spine a testament to years of quiet devotion. "I just want to sing the way that feels true."

Walter nodded, his eyes crinkling at the corners. "Then sing like it's a gift—not a performance."

Callie sat a little taller in her chair, his words lifting something inside her. No questions about her ambition, no suggestions for improvement or exposure. Just permission to be authentic. For the first time since rehearsal, she felt certain of something—not what she would do, exactly, but who she would be while doing it.

The rehearsal room door creaked as Callie entered. Empty chairs stood in their familiar rows, the piano waited like a held breath. The fluorescent lights softly hummed overhead. Rehearsal wasn't scheduled for another forty minutes—precisely why she'd wanted to be here early. She needed the quiet, the chance to remember why she sang in the first place.

The back door swung open with a bang and her mom bustled in, a garment bag slung over one shoulder. "I figured you'd be here already. I've picked up three wardrobe options for Sunday."

Callie's shoulders tensed. Her moment of solitude evaporated like morning dew.

Mom unzipped the garment bag and pulled out a pale blue blouse, holding it up with a flourish.

The fabric caught the light, revealing a subtle shimmer.

"This one's my favorite," mom said, holding it against Callie's shoulders. "See how the neckline will hit right at your collarbone? It'll photograph better than the tops you usually wear. You need to look the part."

"It's fine," Callie said.

"You don't want to see the others? Okay, I really do love this one. Also, when you hit that high note in the second verse, tilt your chin up just a bit." Mom demonstrated with her own head. "Like this. And try to smile—you always look so serious when you sing. And I spoke with Ms. Jenner about adding some dynamics. A little more punch in the middle —something to wow the room."

Each suggestion soured Callie's mood further and further. Especially changing the arrangement of the familiar hymn—the one Walter had taught her, with notes that flowed like water over smooth stones—felt wrong. Like someone had taken a family photograph and airbrushed out the imperfections that made it real.

"What do you think?" Mom's eyes sparkled with excitement.

Callie didn't reply, she really didn't need to. She just nodded, and mom was off to the next topic on her agenda.

Callie felt herself hardening with every suggestion, every comment, every direction.

Eventually, Ms. Jenner entered, her sensible

shoes squeaking against the polished floor. Other choir members began to filter in as well, and Mom was forced to relent and settle in the back of the room. Callie slid into her usual spot, grateful for the reprieve as the director organized her sheet music.

"Alright everyone, let's begin with our big number. We're adjusting things a bit. Callie will still take the solo and we'll all join for the chorus, but watch the dynamics."

The piano notes rippled and danced through the air without the familiar syncopation she loved. Her pulse quickened as she stepped forward.

She gathered herself and began. The first few notes came out clear enough, but as she followed the revised rhythm and approached the crescendo Mom had insisted on, something inside her rebelled. Her voice cracked mid-note, the sound splitting jaggedly through the room before wavering into silence.

Thirty pairs of eyes fixed on her.

"You okay, Callie?" Ms. Jenner asked, her expression gentle.

Before Callie could answer, mom stood. "Probably dry throat. She's fine. Let's just run it again."

Heat crawled up Callie's neck. The embarrassment burned not because she'd failed to hit the note, but because she no longer recognized the performance as her own. This polished, dynamic version felt like a stranger's voice coming from her throat.

The choir director gave Callie an apologetic look. "From the top, please," she said.

Callie stood up taller, pulling her shoulders back. This time, she focused solely on the technical aspects—breath control, pitch accuracy, the exact phrasing Ms. Jenner had marked in pencil. The notes came out clean and precise, her voice moving through the revised melody like someone following a map without looking at the scenery.

She kept her eyes fixed on the sheet music, counting measures, watching for dynamic markings. The crescendo approached. She executed it flawlessly, her voice swelling on command, hitting the high note with technical precision.

The sound that emerged was perfect. And empty.

Behind the pristine delivery, Callie felt nothing —no connection to the sacred words, no warmth flowing through her chest. The hymn that once felt like a prayer now felt like an assignment. She gripped the music folder tighter, knuckles whitening as she finished the verse, her voice a hollow echo in her mind.

The last note faded into silence, unanswered and unresolved. The choir's faces blurred into a sea of expectant smiles. Ms. Jenner nodded with professional approval.

"Thank you," Callie managed, her throat suddenly gone dry. "Excuse me, I need—" She hurried toward the door.

The hallway stretched before her. Callie pushed through the bathroom door, locked herself in the farthest stall, and pressed her forehead against the cool tile wall. The chill seeped into her skin, grounding her when everything else felt wrong.

Emotion caught low in her throat. Her vision blurred with the tears welling in her eyes.

What had happened? The hymn that once connected her to something larger than herself—to Walter, to her own truth, to God—had been transformed into a performance piece. Polished. Perfected. And utterly hollow.

She tasted resentment like bile. She'd let this happen. Note by note, suggestion by suggestion, she'd surrendered what made the music meaningful. She hid while choir practice continued.

Callie slipped from the bathroom stall, splashed cold water on her face, and stared at her reflection. The girl looking back seemed like a stranger—someone caught between who she was and who everyone expected her to be.

She made her way to the fellowship hall, the distant buzz of voices growing louder with each step. Paper plates rattled, and laughter bounced off the walls as she entered the room. Long tables lined with refreshments stood against one wall, youth group members clustered in small groups around them.

Samantha spotted her from across the room and waved enthusiastically. "Callie! Over here!"

Callie picked up a cookie from the dessert table and crossed to join Samantha and Amber.

"You killed that solo," Amber said, leaning forward. "My mom's bringing, like, our entire extended family to hear you."

"The church is gonna be packed," Samantha added, flipping her hair back. "Pastor Mike said they're even setting up extra chairs in the foyer."

"And don't forget the livestream," Madison added, joining them. "My grandma in Florida watches every Easter."

Callie nodded, breaking her cookie into smaller pieces without eating any.

"I told my brother to screenshot the livestream," Samantha said. "If I show up—I'm reposting it everywhere!"

"Better touch up before your solo," Madison nudged Callie's arm. "You never know when they'll zoom in for a close-up."

Callie shifted in her seat, tucking a strand of hair behind her ear. The cookie lay forgotten on her napkin, reduced to a pile of crumbs. She forced her lips into what she hoped resembled a smile, but her hands remained folded tightly in her lap.

"Do you ever feel like it's becoming more about the reaction than the reason?" The words were barely a whisper but they landed in the center of the table like a stone in still water.

The chatter dimmed. Amber's smile faltered.

Samantha tilted her head, her expression open but confused. "Well … the attention just means people are listening, right?"

Callie nodded faintly. Around her, the conversation drifted back to normal—Madison described her Easter dress, Amber debated which songs the praise band might play.

Sunlight streamed through the stained glass windows, casting jewel-toned patterns across the packed sanctuary. Easter lilies adorned the altar, their fragrance rising like incense into the high-ceilinged stillness. In the choir room adjoining the sanctuary, choir members whispered encouragement and last-minute reminders.

Callie stood apart from the others and focused on slowing her pulse, willing her body into a rhythm that might calm the flutter in her stomach. The pages beneath her fingers felt cool and familiar—a contrast to her thoughts, which tumbled and twisted like leaves in a storm.

Mom appeared at her side, perfume announcing her arrival before her voice did.

"Remember what we practiced—strong opening, eye contact with the back row, and that little crescendo we added." Her hands moved to Callie's hair, tucking loose strands behind her ears, smoothing imaginary wrinkles from her shoulders."

Callie nodded, her gaze fixed on a point beyond her mother's shoulder.

Mom's voice dropped to an excited whisper, her eyes bright with anticipation. "This is the moment, baby—let them remember your name." She embraced Callie quickly, then smoothed away imaginary wrinkles from Callie's top.

"I just want to sing from the heart," Callie replied softly, her voice barely audible above the pre-service commotion.

The words hung between them—mom's pushing out, Callie's pulling inward. Neither wrong, but moving in completely different directions.

The choir director motioned for everyone to line up. Callie leaned against the cool wall for a moment longer, pressing her palms flat against its smooth surface as if to absorb something steady, then stepped away from her mother's orbit.

"Sing like it's a gift, not a performance," she whispered, Walter's words becoming her anchor.

In her mind, she returned to his room at Willow Creek—sunlight filtering through thin curtains, the worn hymnal resting in his lap, pages yellowed with time and use. The way his eyes had crinkled at the corners when she sang. The perfect stillness they'd shared after the last note faded.

No cameras. No audience. Just truth passing between them.

The flutter in her stomach had settled. Her shoulders relaxed. Whatever happened next—whether her voice soared or broke—she knew why she was singing. And for whom.

Ms. Jenner signaled, and the choir filed into the sanctuary. Callie found her familiar place, surrounded by the gentle press of bodies and rustling robes.

The sanctuary looked drastically different packed with attendees. There was a din undertone from the gathered crowd. The expectation was palpable.

As the concert began, the choir's voices rose in harmony, filling the space with the first strains of a familiar hymn that vibrated through the wooden floor beneath her feet and grounded Callie once again. The music moved through her like a current, each note washing over her like water, steadying her from the inside out. She gave herself up to it completely and let herself float away in the moment—in release, in worship.

As each song ended, the applause and praise felt right, like a fitting reaction. The focus was not on one individual, but a community blending and worshiping together.

Her song arrived. When Ms. Jenner nodded toward her, signaling her moment, the sanctuary seemed to grow both larger and smaller at once.

She stepped forward. Her shoes made a soft echo against the wooden floor, a private sound amid the silence of expectation. From the corner of her eye, she caught the red glow of mom's phone camera, recording from the front pew.

Callie took the microphone from its stand and looked past the expectant faces, past the flowers and colored light. The reworked piano introduction began.

"Wait, please." The microphone echoed her voice across the crowd.

A hush rippled through the sanctuary, folding in around her like a held note. Without waiting for the piano, she began to sing in her own tempo —gentler, softer, slower than rehearsed. The notes came not from her throat but somewhere deeper, as if drawn from the ground beneath her feet. She didn't try to fill the sanctuary with volume; she didn't strive to be the center of attention. Instead, she let her voice create a quiet center, a still point ringing truer than any crescendo.

The familiar hymn flowed through her, each word carrying the weight of generations who had sung it before. Callie didn't look at the congregation, though she felt their collective gaze. She didn't seek out the cameras that were livestreaming this moment. She didn't check her mother's face for the disappointment that she knew must be there. Instead, she focused inward, to the quiet place where music lived before it became sound.

Her hands relaxed at her sides. The tension in her shoulders dissolved. Each phrase emerged pure and unadorned—no vocal runs, no dramatic swells where they didn't belong. Just the melody, carried on something deeper than sound, as if it moved through her rather than from her.

The sanctuary's acoustics embraced her voice, carrying it to the rafters without strain. Ms. Jenner at the piano began a gentle accompaniment, following Callie's lead. Callie sensed rather than saw the subtle shift in the room. Not the reaction of an audience impressed by skill, but of people drawn into presence.

This was Walter's gift to her—understanding that music wasn't something you performed but something you shared. Something you became.

As she approached the final verse, a calm certainty filled her entire being. The piano dropped out for the final few words, and she delivered them acapella. The last note rose from her, clear and unwavering, lingering like light filtered through stained glass.

Callie let the silence that followed become part of the song itself. She stood within it, still and open, holding the moment before it slipped away.

The silence felt shared, like everyone in the room sensed something too sacred to interrupt. No one coughed. No programs rustled. The sanctuary remained utterly still, suspended in that fragile space between ending and after.

She didn't need to open her eyes to feel it —the reverence woven into the silence, different from applause but somehow more significant. This wasn't the awkward pause before reluctant recognition. This was communion.

When the clapping finally began, it rose like a gentle tide—hesitant at first, then swelling. Callie's gaze drifted to the front pew where mom sat, her hands moving together more slowly than those around her. Her mother's expression had shifted from the tight anticipation of before to something softer, more wondering.

Callie didn't bow. Didn't smile for effect. She simply replaced the microphone with steady hands, her shoulders straight but not rigid. The weight that had dragged on her for weeks had lifted, replaced by a quiet certainty.

She hadn't conquered the room. She'd found herself within it.

Callie slipped into the hallway, her choir folder pressed against her side like a shield. The sanctuary doors stood propped open behind her, but she moved far enough away that the voices became a gentle hum rather than distinct words.

The wall felt cool against her back as she leaned against it. She drew in a long breath scented with Easter lilies and furniture polish.

The rest of the concert had buoyed her. After her solo, she'd surrendered fully—lost in worship, not performance.

The murmur of conversation continued in the sanctuary. What had happened in there belonged to them now. It was something they all shared. What she'd felt while singing belonged only to her, but it had created an authentic experience that would affect everyone who had been in the room, or been watching the livestream.

Footsteps echoed down the corridor, the sharp click-click of heels against tile growing louder. Her mother rounded the corner, practically vibrating with excitement. Mom's cheeks flushed pink, her eyes bright with a familiar gleam that made Callie's stomach tighten.

"There you are!" Mom clasped her hands together. "You had them, Cal. The whole room. We could really do something with this."

Callie was disappointed as her mother's words tumbled out in a rush. She had hoped her mom had finally understood. She had hoped the experience had helped her understand.

"Pastor Reed's wife knows someone at Berklee —can you imagine? And we should get you proper recordings, not just phone videos. Maybe look into some—"

The hallway seemed to shrink. Callie stared at the floor tiles, counting speckles just to stay grounded. What made it excruciating was how real her mother's joy was. Real and warm and completely rooted in something Callie had never asked for.

"Mom." The word escaped her lips as a whisper at first, then with more strength. "Mom."

Mom paused mid-sentence, the last of her

words trailing into a quiet that felt suddenly weighty.

"I don't want to build something around being seen." The words formed themselves, truth crystallizing as she spoke. "I don't want to sing for notice or recognition. Maybe that's something you wanted, but it's not what I want ... it's not who I am."

Her heart hammered against her ribs, but her voice didn't waver. This wasn't rebellion or rejection—just the quiet unfurling of who she was, who she'd always been beneath the noise. The air between them felt fragile, as if something precious balanced there, waiting to be recognized.

Mom's hands dropped to her sides, the frenetic energy that had propelled her words now stilled. She studied Callie's face with an intensity that felt different from before—not searching for potential or planning next steps, but actually seeing her daughter.

The silence stretched between them, punctuated only by distant voices from the sanctuary. Callie waited, her breath shallow, still clutching her choir folder.

"I wanted this for you ... I wanted this for both of us." Mom's voice came softer now, a note of vulnerability creeping in. "I thought ... I thought this could be everything for you."

"It already was," Callie said, her voice gentle but unwavering. "But not because of what comes next."

Mom's lips parted slightly, then closed. She looked to the floor, then back to Callie's face. She didn't argue. She clasped Callie's hands, gave them a gentle pat, and pulled her daughter into a tight embrace.

Walter's door stood slightly ajar. Callie nudged it open without knocking, a privilege earned through years of visits. The room smelled of lilies and aftershave, the Easter flowers standing tall in a simple glass vase beside his worn leather Bible.

Walter sat in his armchair, eyes closed, breathing deep and even. Callie slipped into the empty chair beside him and reached for his hand, her fingers sliding into his weathered palm.

He woke from his afternoon doze. "Well, I didn't expect to see you here today. Thought you'd be too busy signing autographs and scheduling interviews!"

"I think if Mom could have her way, we would be, but we talked. I think we're better now. I wish you would have been there. After I finished singing, there was this moment ... No one moved. No one said a word. That silence ... it felt full."

"I was there in spirit. And I watched the whole thing on the TV in the Activity Room." He nodded slowly, voice rough with sleep but warm with understanding. "That's the sound of honesty and truth taking root. I felt it, Callie. I couldn't see every detail, but I felt it. It was clear. And it was yours."

The words grounded her, steady and sure. "It was just … amazing."

Walter tapped his cane twice against the floor. "Truth has a different resonance. It doesn't need to shout to be really heard."

Walter leaned forward slightly, his eyes crinkling at the corners. Callie pressed his hand gently. No need to fill the space with words when understanding already bridged the gap between them.

A light knock broke the stillness. Mom stood in the doorway, still in her Easter dress, a soft hesitancy in her posture that Callie rarely saw. Their eyes met briefly before mom's gaze took in the tableau of grandfather and granddaughter.

Mom stepped into the room, the click of her heels muted against the carpet. She placed a hand on Callie's shoulder, her touch light but steady.

"Dad, her performance was beautiful," she said after a beat, taking Walter's other hand and forming a circle between them. "It was honest."

The words landed like a truce, temporary maybe, but real enough to breathe in. It didn't fix everything, but it felt like the first time her mom saw her instead of the dream she could become.

In the quiet that followed, Callie felt the same fullness she'd experienced after her final note—that suspended moment before the applause. For her, this was the perfect finish. This was the note she wanted to hold long after the music faded.

Seasoned With Wisdom

*E*sther observed the spectacle from the kitchen
doorway, absently twisting her apron strings
between her fingers. In all her years working in
kitchens, she'd never seen one turned into a modeling
studio.

Diego stood with his arms crossed, the knot of
his jet-black kitchen bandana tight at the nape of
his neck. He watched over Marcus' right shoulder
as he framed another shot.

"Rotate the plate six degrees left," Diego
instructed as if the photographer didn't know how
to compose an image.

Diego reached past and used his tweezers to
adjust a single microgreen on the beet foam
creation—a dish no resident here at Willow
Creek Retirement Village had ever requested—or
finished.

She glanced again at the bus cart of meals
behind her loaded with tonight's dinners, waiting

for Chef's approval to go out and getting cold while this ... performance ... continued.

"I'm sure this one will be selected for the Family Weekend brochure," Marcus said with approval.

Diego's slight nod carried more satisfaction than Esther had seen when people actually ate his food.

"Can these go out now, Chef?" she asked.

"Yes ... yes." He waved without even glancing in her direction.

Esther took a deep breath, straightened her back, and pushed through the double doors to the dining room. The weight of the cart with Diego's artistic creations felt heavier than usual. Not from physical strain—her arms had pushed countless carts and carried countless trays over decades—but from what she knew would follow.

She set the first plate before Doris, a retired librarian with soft eyes and papery hands.

"Is it dessert or dinner?" Doris squinted at the pink foam dotted with twigs, her fork hovering uncertainly.

"It's roasted beet mousse with goat cheese crumble," Esther explained, trying to summon enthusiasm she didn't feel. "Chef says it's very ... contemporary."

Ray, seated across from Doris, prodded his portion with his fork. The tines left tiny tracks in the foam that immediately began to collapse. "I like beets, but I still have teeth. I don't need them pureed."

Esther moved to the next table, setting down more plates. The residents' faces fell one by one.

"I think I've met a mousse before, up in the Rockies," quipped Carl. "They don't look a thing like this!" A few chuckles rippled through the room.

Walter, who'd been asking for meatloaf for three weeks, snorted. "He's not cooking for us. He's interviewing for his next restaurant job. That camera in there is his résumé."

Esther's chest tightened as she watched the resident's hands retreat from utensils. Their mouths, that should be chewing, formed thin lines instead. They exchanged glances—not angry, just disappointed. Hungry.

Esther recognized the glances from her last days working in the high school cafeteria when budget cuts meant serving processed food instead of the from-scratch meals she'd once prided herself on. Kids complained about cafeteria food no matter what, but when it became 'bad' cafeteria food, and they backed up their complaints by throwing it away untouched, Esther had felt horrible.

"I'll see if there's some bread in the kitchen," she whispered to Doris, patting her shoulder gently.

Esther collected the plates, each one a small tragedy of untouched or slightly picked-over food. Doris had taken two polite bites before setting her fork down. Ray hadn't even attempted. The pink foam had collapsed entirely, the microgreens wilting like abandoned houseplants.

Oscar was the only one who had cleaned his plate entirely, proving once again that he would eat anything.

At the next table, six more plates waited—identical stories of hunger unmet. She placed them in the bus tub with a gentleness that belied her frustration. Good ingredients shouldn't go to waste like this. People shouldn't go to bed hungry.

She carried the tub back through the kitchen, her steps measured but deliberate. The junior prep cook glanced up from his station, eyes meeting hers before quickly darting away. He knew. They all knew.

Esther grabbed a rag and attacked a prep counter, scrubbing circles with more force than the spotless surface required. Thirty years. Thirty years she'd spent in that high school cafeteria, watching kids grow up bite by bite. They'd grumbled about her meatloaf too, but they'd always cleaned their plates. They'd come back for seconds.

This job was supposed to be temporary. A stopgap after the district cuts. But she'd hoped it would be as rewarding as the high school job had been–meeting people's need for food, as well as making connections, growing together.

Now she felt like a museum docent, serving art no one wanted to consume.

It wasn't Diego, not really. It was this whole charade of pretending that beautiful meant nourishing. Pretending that elderly people needed to be impressed rather than fed. It would be different if these were diners choosing a dining experience; willing participants instead of voiceless casualties.

Esther stacked the plates in the dishwasher, each clink a small protest against the evening's culinary disappointment. Behind her, Marcus and Diego discussed the photos and intricacies of the plates.

"Look at this one," Marcus said, holding his camera toward Diego. "This angle really highlights the vertical composition."

Diego leaned in, his pristine chef's whites still immaculate despite hours in the kitchen. Not a single splash or stain—Esther wondered if he actually cooked or just arranged.

"It's all about balance. Elevation. Color dynamics." His voice carried the rehearsed demeanor of someone who practiced talking points in mirrors.

Esther returned the empty tray to the sink. She slid past them without pausing, but couldn't hold her tongue any longer.

"They won't eat a marketing brochure either," she said, loud enough for both to hear.

Marcus managed to keep his surprise to a slight raise of his eyebrows. Diego turned slowly, his practiced smile thinning into something sharp.

"Not everyone understands fine dining," he said softly, but not kindly.

Esther dried her hands on her apron, eyes fixed on the growing mound of wasted food. Something shifted inside her—a quiet certainty replacing weeks of uncomfortable doubt. This wasn't just wrong; it was fixable. These residents deserved better than beautiful hunger.

After finally getting the dining room cleaned and reset, feet aching from her long shift, Esther was glad to be done for the day. She was walking towards the employee parking lot when hushed voices over the soft hum of the vending machine motor stopped her.

"Got any quarters left, Walter?"

"Here, Martha. Get the peanut butter ones— they're filling."

Esther paused to listen to the residents gathered in the vending alcove ahead. The clink of coins and mechanical whirring confirmed what she already knew: Diego's artful plates had sent the residents searching for something to tide them over.

She edged forward and peeked around the corner, watching as they shared packaged crackers and whispered complaints. The fluorescent lights cast a harsh glow over Walter as he meticulously peeled the wrapper from a granola bar, treating the simple snack with the reverence of a five-star dessert.

"Care to join our little rebellion, Esther?" Carl extended his hand, offering a peanut butter pretzel. "We've got quite the spread tonight."

She hesitated, but then joined them by the machine. "I can't take your pretzels, Carl, but thank you. You all shouldn't have to sneak around for food."

"We're not sneaking," said Carl. "We're foraging!"

Merry popped a chocolate chip into her mouth and hummed with satisfaction. "Better than the beet foam, that's for certain. What was that supposed to be, anyway? Looked like something that washed up on shore during red tide."

Walter chuckled. "Now Esther, you have to promise not to disclose our little Vending Machine Communion. Deal?"

She nodded.

"Reminds me of fishing trips," Carl said, cracking his knuckles. "Best meals I ever had were beans heated over a campfire, stars overhead."

"Lemon bars were the only thing I could ever cook. Good thing I got free meals after my sets on the cruise ship," Merry said, nodding, her scarf swaying. Then she added in a sing-song voice: "If I knew you were comin' I'd've baked a cake, hired a band, goodness sake!"

"Come see something," Carl whispered, beckoning her with a crooked finger.

The small group shuffled around the corner, huddling near the swinging kitchen doors. Through the round window, Esther spotted Diego in his pristine whites, hunched over a single plate at the prep station. His phone hovered above the dish as he adjusted a garnish with tweezers, turning the plate a quarter-inch before snapping another photo.

"Been at it for twenty minutes," Walter murmured. "Same plate."

A pang hit as Diego meticulously positioned each element, his face tightening with concentration. He stepped back, considered the arrangement, then leaned in to adjust a sauce droplet with the tip of his finger.

Carl shook his head, his voice gravel-rough. "He's feeding his camera better than he feeds us."

Walter tapped his cane twice against the floor. "Plenty of knowledge. Not enough seasoning."

Esther leaned against the wall, watching the residents share their makeshift meal. She tucked a loose strand of hair back into her bun. Diego's meals met the required nutritional guidelines, but if nobody would eat them, did it matter? The foods the residents remembered, the foods they craved, could meet those guidelines too.

"What foods do you miss most?" she asked finally, her voice soft. "If you could cook anything tomorrow, what would it be?"

Carl's eyes lit up. "My lake trout. Caught fresh, scaled right there on shore. Just butter, lemon, and thyme stuffed inside. Wrap it in foil, nestle it in the campfire coals. Twenty minutes, not a second more."

Merry closed her eyes. "Hmmmm ... Something sweet ... not any particular thing, just that taste ... smooth, sweet ... velvety ..." She trailed off, smiling.

Walter laced his fingers together, his blue eyes thoughtful. "Half of it is the food, but the other half is who you're with, and the conversations you're having ..." He paused, frowning. "Wait, is that three halves?"

They all laughed, and Esther felt something warm unfurling inside her—a sense of purpose she hadn't felt since leaving the high school.

She told the residents good night and headed for the staff parking lot. Just before she pushed through the door, however, laughter echoed down the hall from the vending machine alcove. Real joy. For her, that brought to mind food. Not of fancy foams or artful smears, but she thought of casseroles and cobblers, hand passed across tables. Food that filled more than stomachs–what these people actually needed.

The activity room felt cavernous in its emptiness—just rows of folding chairs circling a long table, the walls lined with craft bins and faded puzzle boxes. Esther set the ladle down and adjusted the checkered tablecloth on the card table, smoothing out a wrinkle. The tomato soup's fragrance was a counterpoint to the smell of industrial cleaner and that peculiar staleness unique to rooms that were regularly sanitized but rarely lived in.

The stockpot of tomato soup gently simmered on one hot plate, while grilled cheese sandwiches slowly browned on a skillet atop another. Nothing fancy—nothing Diego would ever photograph—just honest food that smelled like comfort.

Allen Carter, the executive director at Willow Creek, checked his watch for the third time in as many minutes. His tie was perfectly knotted, but his mouth formed a tight line.

"Just make sure this doesn't ... become a thing," he said, voice clipped.

"It's just soup," Esther replied with a small smile, though her stomach knotted.

"Diego wasn't informed. Let's keep it low-profile." Mr. Carter's eyes darted around the empty room as if searching for witnesses. "You've got an hour."

He nodded curtly and left, the door clicking shut behind him.

Alone, Esther exhaled a breath she hadn't realized she'd been holding. She picked up the wooden spoon and stirred the soup slowly, watching the gentle swirl of red. What if nobody came? She would be as bad as Diego, wasting all this food–luckily, she was sure hers cost a lot less than his. She'd paid for it herself, after all.

She'd pitched the idea of a 'Comfort Food Social' to Allen as an activity for the residents, not a meal. And she'd selected the Activity room because it was as far away from the dining room and kitchen as she could get.

Her intention wasn't to challenge Diego, or to upset him ... She just wanted to meet the residents' needs.

She stirred the soup and waited, straining to hear footsteps in the hallway.

She arranged the mismatched mugs in a semicircle—chipped ceramics bearing faded vacation spots and inspirational quotes. She placed paper bowls and plates beside them, then tucked napkins into an old coffee tin.

She adjusted the handwritten sign: "Tomato Soup & Grilled Cheese—just like home." The letters looked childish, nothing like Diego's elegant menu cards. She considered pitching it into the trash, but resisted.

A second pan of grilled cheese sizzled, the bread a shade darker than she'd aimed for. She flipped the sandwiches, breathing in the warm, buttery aroma. At least it smelled right.

Ten minutes had passed. The clock ticked. No shuffling feet, no voices in the hall.

Doubt settled in her chest like a stone. Maybe holding this after dinner was too late in the evening for the residents. Maybe she had misinterpreted what was going on, and people were okay with the job Diego was doing ... maybe they were satisfied.

She glanced toward the hallway, taking a breath and unclenching her jaw.

The door creaked open. Esther stopped mid-stir as Carl poked his head in, nostrils flaring slightly. His weathered face brightened as he stepped fully into the room.

"Well now," he said, inhaling deeply. "Smells like my daughter's first apartment. Kitchen the size of a closet, but she could sure make soup."

Relief flooded through Esther's body, warm as the soup she'd been stirring. Her shoulders relaxed as she ladled the tomato soup into a paper bowl.

"Here you go," she said, handing him both the soup and a plate with grilled cheese. The smile she offered alongside them felt more genuine than any she'd shared in weeks.

Carl settled into a folding chair with a satisfied grunt. He dipped a corner of sandwich into the soup and took a bite, closing his eyes momentarily.

"You always cook like this?" he asked, gesturing to the simple spread.

Esther wiped her hands on her apron, suddenly aware of how basic everything looked. "Only when I'm nervous," she admitted.

Her heart swelled as the door swung open again. Merry glided in with theatrical grace, her colorful scarf trailing behind her as she swung her hips slightly to the tune she was humming.

"Hey good lookin', what ya got cookin' ..."

Merry's melodic voice filled the room as she approached the table. Her eyes lit up at the sight of the soup and sandwiches. "Well, isn't this a delightful surprise!"

Walter's arrival announced itself with the rhythmic tap-tap of his cane against the linoleum floor. He entered with dignified posture despite his stoop, blue eyes twinkling as he surveyed the scene.

"I was promised comfort food, not artwork," he declared, the corners of his mouth twitching upward. "About time someone remembered what food is supposed to be."

Relief washed over Esther as she moved between the hot plates, ladling soup with one hand while flipping sandwiches with the other.

"The bread might be a touch dark on some," she said apologetically, sliding a plate toward Walter.

"Perfect," he countered, breaking the sandwich in half to release a stream of melted cheese. "Crisp edges are the point."

As they ate, something in the room shifted. The institutional chill gave way to something warmer, more lived-in. Carl launched into his trout stories —the one about the midnight catch during the thunderstorm—and this time, laughter rippled through the small gathering.

Merry dabbed her lips with a napkin and closed her eyes, humming a few notes before breaking into a soft verse—"Flour on the table, sugar in the bowl ..." She swayed slightly. "My mother sang that while making her famous apple cake."

Ray and Doris joined, as did Frank.

Esther felt herself relax, wooden spoon in hand, no longer just serving but belonging. The nervous hostess had vanished, replaced by something she hadn't felt yet here at Willow Creek —the quiet confidence of knowing exactly what people needed.

Esther stirred the nearly empty pot, the metal spoon scraping gently against the bottom. The warmth in her heart had nothing to do with the hot plates and everything to do with the contented murmurs around her.

"I wasn't sure anyone would come," she admitted, setting the spoon down. "I pitched this to the administration last week. I thought they'd shut it down immediately."

Walter tapped his cane against the floor, a knowing smile crossing his face. "That's how you know it's worth doing, my dear. The best ideas always feel a little risky."

Carl wiped his mouth with a napkin, the corners of his eyes crinkling. "So when's the next one? Thursday, maybe?" He leaned forward, eager as a child. "Been thinking about my wife's corn chowder recipe. Could write it down for you."

Esther's hand froze mid-reach for a dirty mug. She hadn't thought past today, hadn't dared imagine this becoming regular. The question caught her off-guard, like an unexpected gift.

"I ... I don't know," she stammered, something

fragile and hopeful fluttering in her chest. "Would you want that? Another gathering? I'm not sure Mr. Carter will go for it."

The chorus of enthusiastic nods made her throat tighten. She felt needed again, and felt she was meeting a need as well.

"This certainly beats the vending machine," Merry said.

Esther wiped her hands on her apron, blinking back the moisture welling in her eyes. The second pot of soup sat nearly empty, just a thin red film coating the bottom. Empty paper bowls stacked in the garbage told the story of success better than words could.

"What about a chili night next week?" Carl suggested, eyes bright with anticipation.

Walter raised an eyebrow. "With your spice tolerance? We'd need a medical team on standby."

Esther nodded slowly, her smile genuine but her mind already elsewhere. She wasn't just planning another meal—she was rebuilding something she'd thought lost forever.

Esther shifted in her uncomfortable plastic chair, trying not to check the clock on the wall. The monthly staff meeting dragged on like a voicemail transcription—full of awkward pauses and nothing worth hearing.

Allen Carter stood at the head of the table,

sleeves rolled to three-quarter length, tapping his pen on his leather portfolio.

"Excellent work on the garden pathway repairs," he nodded to the facilities team. "Lisa, any updates from housekeeping?"

A tired-looking woman in a facilities polo flipped through her notes. "Three of our staff are out with the flu—it's going around. But we've maintained our metrics: thirty-two loads of laundry daily, average room cleaning time holding at seventeen minutes."

Esther paused from doodling flowers on her meeting agenda and winced. Seventeen minutes to clean someone's entire living space? How sanitized could that be?

When Allen called for food and nutrition feedback, Diego straightened further in his chair. "The kitchen served 2,784 plates this month, with presentation scores averaging 9.2 out of 10 from website visitors." He swiped through his phone, turning it to display a perfectly arranged plate. "Our plating techniques continue to receive social media engagement well above industry standards."

Esther set her pen down and cleared her throat. "The Comfort Food Social has seen participation increase by forty percent since we started." Her voice sounded thin in the corporate conference room. "Only been two meetings, but folks are participating instead of heading to the vending machines, so that's good."

Diego's jaw tightened. "Grilled cheese isn't exactly culinary innovation. It's low-bar hospitality at best."

The room fell silent. Esther's cheeks flushed.

"Maybe so. But I've watched Mr. Peterson eat a full meal for the first time in months. They're sharing stories about family recipes, reconnecting with food memories." Esther found herself pushing down on the table, spreading her fingers wide. "Sometimes people just need to remember why eating matters in the first place."

She began folding the agenda paper into progressively smaller rectangles, needing something to ground herself. The conference room suddenly felt smaller, the fluorescent lights harsher.

"This is absurd," Diego said, his accent sharpening with each word. "These socials undermine everything we're trying to accomplish in the dining program. We have standards, techniques—"

"We have hungry residents," Esther countered, her voice steadier than she felt.

Diego's face flushed. "We're not running a nostalgia café. The goal isn't to coddle their memories—it's to expand their palates, give them something new. Attract attention."

Esther felt something snap inside her—thirty years of lunch lady patience finally giving way.

"Expand their palates? They're not your Instagram followers or editors from Food and

Wine Magazine, Diego. They're people who've lived full lives and know what they want." She leaned forward. "Your beautiful plates go straight to the trash while they eat vending machine snacks at night."

"That's their choice! Their failure to appreciate culinary evolution!" Diego shook his head in disgust. "What's next—we serve SpaghettiOs because someone's mother made it when they skinned their knee?"

"If it makes them eat, yes!" Esther felt her neck grow hot. "You create art for a marketing brochure while ignoring the actual people you're meant to feed."

"I didn't train for fifteen years to make grilled cheese sandwiches," Diego hissed.

"And they didn't live seventy years to be your test kitchen," Esther shot back.

Mr. Carter brought his hand down on the table flat, the crack silencing the room. "That's enough, both of you."

Esther's temples throbbed with her pulse. She hadn't lost her temper like that since the school board tried cutting free lunches back in '09.

Allen flipped a few pages in his portfolio. "It just so happens that I have the latest quarterly survey results here." He cleared his throat. "Regarding dining services: 'Too fancy to chew. I miss meatloaf.' 'This isn't the food I grew up on.' 'I can't pronounce half the menu items.' 'This isn't food for people my age.'"

Esther watched Diego's face. His expression remained composed, but his fingers drummed rapidly against his phone.

"Family Weekend is in three weeks," Allen continued. "If residents are complaining to their children about the food ..." He let the implication hang.

Esther felt a pang of sympathy despite herself. Diego looked like someone had just questioned his citizenship.

"Our retention numbers depend on family satisfaction," Allen said. "If they hear their parents aren't eating properly, we risk losing residents to facilities with more ... traditional menus."

Esther watched Diego's face transform, his eyes narrowed as he leaned forward and adjusted his already straight collar.

"If they want comfort food, then I'll give them that, but reimagined comfort food. Elevated. Elegant." He emphasized each word as if explaining a complex concept to a child. "We can maintain standards while addressing their preferences."

Esther sighed, feeling the weight of thirty years serving students who just needed nourishment, not performance art.

"Or maybe what they want doesn't need reimagining," she said quietly. "Sometimes grilled cheese is just perfect, as is."

Allen rubbed the bridge of his nose. "Here's what we'll do. Family Weekend will feature Diego's menu—elevated comfort classics. But Esther, you can continue your socials—for now. We'll reassess based on resident feedback."

Esther watched Allen lean back in his chair, rubbing his eyes beneath his glasses. The executive director looked caught between corporate metrics and actual human needs.

"Meeting adjourned," he sighed.

Diego stood and marched right, toward the kitchen, his shoes clicking against the polished floor. Esther slid her folded agenda into her purse and shuffled out, turning left toward the dining room. Neither looked at the other. Neither had won. The residents would continue to be caught in their tug-of-war, pulled between artistry and nourishment, between what looked good and what felt good.

In the days that followed, Diego continued his culinary assault on the residents, unwaveringly featuring torchons, tuiles, crudo, and foams. The day before the big dinner, however, Esther watched the kitchen unravel before her eyes. The whiteboard resembled a battlefield, names crossed out with harsh strokes of red marker. Five kitchen staff down with the flu that had been creeping through the facility. She stood quietly by the pantry, hands clasped tightly behind her back, taking in Diego's frantic energy as he paced the line.

"That's six messages now. No one's responding." Diego's phone clutched in his white-knuckled grip. "We're down to two—maybe."

Mr. Carter stood nearby, arms crossed tightly against his chest. His usual composed demeanor cracked around the edges, worry lines deepening across his forehead.

"The Family Weekend Dinner is tomorrow," Allen said, his voice tight. "We have sixty-eight confirmed guests in addition to the residents."

Esther felt the weight of tomorrow pressing down on all of them.

She watched the panic build behind Diego's eyes. Despite his rigid posture and commanding presence, she recognized the subtle tells—the way his fingers twitched against his phone, how his gaze darted between Allen and the empty kitchen stations. She'd seen that look countless times in her cafeteria days when a deadline loomed impossible.

"I'll call around," Diego announced, straightening his pristine chef's coat. "A couple of my contacts teach at culinary programs. We can get some externs in."

Allen shook his head, tapping through screens on his tablet. The blue light reflected harshly against his furrowed brow.

"We can't afford outside labor. We've already stretched this event thin; we're way over budget on marketing as it is."

Diego's shoulders stiffened. "Then we'll have to cancel the centerpiece dishes. I can't execute this alone."

Esther noticed how his voice carried an edge of desperation beneath the professional tone. For all his bravado, Diego looked genuinely cornered—a chef without his brigade, facing the impossible choice between perfection and practicality.

She watched the two men fret over the crisis, her mind drifting to the residents gathered around the vending machine just weeks ago. Their weathered hands, once skilled at crafting meals that nourished families for decades, reduced to fumbling with cellophane wrappers. Then to the latest Comfort Food Social, and how everyone had wanted to pitch in. A solution crystallized in her mind, simple and obvious.

"Let the residents help," she said, her voice quiet but firm.

Both men turned toward her. The kitchen fell into complete silence.

Diego's eyebrows shot up, his face a portrait of disbelief. "You're serious?"

Esther nodded, wiping her hands on her apron out of habit. "They want to be involved. They know their way around a kitchen."

Diego scoffed, his arms crossing defensively. "This isn't tuna casserole and potluck night. I'm not risking my station on Carl's fish stories."

Allen looked between them, his expression thoughtful rather than dismissive. "Could it work,

Chef?"

Diego's jaw tightened. "It's doubtful ... but, if —and that's a big if—I allow it, it's under one condition: I train them. They do things my way. They follow my process. No improvising."

"Done," Allen said with sudden decisiveness. "Set up a training session for your volunteers this afternoon between services. Esther, make sure you're only recruiting our capable and willing residents. Diego, can you get today's meals out with the staff you have?"

"We'll make it." he replied.

She watched his fingers tighten around his pen as he scribbled furiously on the notepad. His knuckles whitened with each aggressive stroke.

"If they're touching anything in my kitchen, they'll follow every safety rule, every measurement, and every knife grip exactly," he said, underlining words with such force the paper nearly tore.

"I'll round up the volunteers," Esther offered. "Carl's been waiting for a chance like this. And Merry. Walter too." She could already picture their faces lighting up at the invitation.

Allen clapped his hands once. "Then we're agreed."

His gaze hardened as he turned to Diego. "And Diego—if this goes well, you'll get credit. If it doesn't ... we'll rethink how we handle events going forward."

Diego gave a clipped nod but Esther caught the

flicker of anxiety behind his professional mask.

She stepped out into the hallway, leaving Diego hunched over his recipe binder. Through the small window in the kitchen door, she watched him frantically redrawing arrows between steps, his pen moving with the same exactness he reserved for plating. Only now, his movements carried a desperate edge.

She spotted Carl and Merry chatting by the activity board and approached with a warm smile.

"How would you two feel about a short kitchen training this afternoon?" she asked, her voice gentle. "We could use some extra hands for Family Weekend."

Carl's weathered face brightened. Merry's eyes sparkled with interest.

"About time someone asked," Carl said.

Hanging back by the doorway, Esther watched the unlikely classroom take shape. The activity room's cheerful bingo charts and crafting supplies had been hastily pushed aside, replaced by folding tables laden with cutting boards and mixing bowls. Diego had taped laminated recipe sheets to the wall arranged by course.

The residents shuffled in with surprising eagerness. Carl arrived first, flexing his fingers as if preparing to scale today's catch. Doris brought her own floral apron, meticulously pressed. Walter moved with judicial deliberation, while Ray hummed softly, tapping rhythm against his thigh. Merry swept in last, oven mitts dangling from a belt loop like colorful ornaments.

Diego stood at the front, his pristine white coat buttoned to perfection, clenched fists resting on his hips. His expression reminded Esther of a pressure cooker about to whistle.

"Let's go. Follow along closely," he clapped once, the sharp sound echoing through the room. "This is a professional kitchen now. If you are working in my kitchen, you'll do things my way to my standards. We'll review those now."

No welcome. No thank-you, Esther thought. He just dove right in with the warmth of a drill instructor.

Diego demonstrated a series of techniques, calling out their names and performing them with practiced precision—herbs folded and sliced into perfect ribbons, vegetables diced into identical cubes, sauces drizzled in symmetrical patterns. His hands moved with the confidence of someone who'd performed these motions thousands of times.

The residents watched with mild interest, but Esther noticed they quickly drifted toward their own rhythms. Carl quietly picked up a potato and began peeling it in one continuous spiral, completely ignoring Diego. Merry hummed a soft lounge melody while sorting utensils on her station.

Doris took her recipe sheet and deliberately refolded it to hide Diego's meticulous annotations. Ray spilled a scoop of flour, but instead of panicking, he hummed softly and brushed it into his palm.

"Okay. Now you begin. Repeat what I've just shown you," Diego said, placing his knife on the cutting board with a snap.

Each resident attempted ... something. There was no skill, no precision. It wasn't rebellion. They simply existed in a different culinary world altogether.

She noticed the tension building in the pressure cooker that was the head chef. The residents' failure to execute his exacting instructions bubbled against his professional pride and she recognized the signs—the tightening around his eyes, the increasingly clipped tone, the way he kept adjusting his already-perfect sleeves.

Walter paused, mid-stir. "Chef, does it really need to be that exact?"

The question hung in the air for only a heartbeat before Diego replied in a loud, clipped voice. "Yes. It does. Because this meal matters. Because there are expectations. Because you can't just ... sing your way through a kitchen!"

Silence. Everyone stopped. Merry's soft tune faded into nothing.

Diego exhaled harshly and stepped away from the counter, eyes darting to the list of tasks taped to the wall. He stared at the list, then shook his head slowly, releasing a long breath.

Esther watched the crack in his armor become a fracture.

He returned to the cutting board and grasped the knife again. "Let's start again with dicing. You'll all watch carefully, then I'll visit each station, and you will dice a tomato to my satisfaction."

"Um ... my tomato's already in the pot," Carl said.

She watched Diego's shoulders slump, his perfect posture crumbling like an overworked pastry. The knife he'd been demonstrating with clattered against the cutting board as he set it down and gripped the edge of the prep table, knuckles whitening.

"You know what?" His voice had lost its edge, replaced by something hollower. "Fine. Do what you want. Make your soups and stews and tell your stories. But tomorrow in the kitchen, no one will touch my station. No one will touch my dish. It will be done correctly. It will be the one thing tomorrow that actually works. You can't be taught ... you won't learn. Fine, you can serve slop. I'll serve perfection."

Diego scowled and stared at Esther. She felt the blame from across the room. He turned and left without another word, slamming the door behind him.

Walter nodded once. Carl just shrugged and

returned to peeling an apple, striving again for a continuous, unbroken peel. Merry's humming resumed, gentler now, like she was trying not to startle a wild rabbit.

Esther just watched, feeling a strange mix of victory and sadness. Diego had declared retreat, building walls around the last piece of control he had. In his mind, he wasn't abandoning ship; he was saving the one treasure worth preserving.

"So, can we just stay here tonight and eat this? We don't have to go down for regular dinner, do we?" Carl asked.

When Esther entered the kitchen, dawn was just breaking over Willow Creek, and Diego was already at his station. He didn't acknowledge her in any way, just continued his preparation.

She tied her apron—the one with the faded sunflower pattern, not the stiff white uniform the facility provided.

Behind her, the residents filed in with quiet purpose. Carl carried a paper bag of fresh herbs, their scent trailing him like a memory. Doris clutched her embroidered pouch of spices, fingers moving over them as if counting rosary beads. Walter entered with his cane tapping a gentle rhythm against the tile. Ray hummed something low and sweet, while Merry's eyes sparkled with anticipation.

"Morning, kitchen crew," Esther said, the words feeling right in her mouth. Not staff, not helpers—crew. Team.

She laid out handwritten cards at each station. "Carl, you're on stew—beef today, no fish ... sorry. Doris, side dishes. Ray—napkin duty and table settings for now, then you'll help out where needed. Walter, you're handling pasta sauce. Merry, you're with me on desserts. We're all wearing hair nets, masks, and gloves today, this is the real deal."

At first, they were hesitant moving around the commercial kitchen, but soon the familiar chatter ensued, and the homey, relaxed atmosphere of a family kitchen settled over them.

The kitchen came alive around her, and that internal relief bloomed on Esther's face. Spoons clinked against bowls, knives tapped against cutting boards, and laughter bubbled up between recipe swaps.

Diego continued working alone, his pristine chef's coat buttoned to the collar despite the kitchen's growing warmth. He didn't acknowledge anyone—not the residents chopping and stirring, not Esther overseeing the operation. His gaze remained fixed on his workstation.

She noticed how deliberately he arranged his tools—tweezers, pipettes, measuring spoons all lined with military precision. His notebook lay open, filled with diagrams that looked more like architectural drawings than recipes. Diego's movements were mechanical, his face a careful blank as he measured truffle oil by the milliliter.

Meanwhile, Carl tossed another handful of thyme into his stew, sniffing appreciatively as the herb hit the simmering broth. Merry's laughter rang out when Ray accidentally dusted his nose with flour. The scent of caramelizing onions and fresh-baked bread wrapped around them all like a warm blanket.

Esther caught Diego pausing mid-slice, his knife hovering as his eyes drifted toward the group. For just a moment, something flickered across his face—not anger or resentment, but something more vulnerable. He looked like a child with his face pressed against a window, watching a party he hadn't been invited to.

Esther's hands fell into the familiar rhythm of rolling dough alongside Merry, her mind drifting between tasks as she kept watch over her kitchen crew. Not her subordinates—her partners. The thought warmed her more than the ovens.

Carl stood hunched over his stew, wooden spoon moving in slow circles as he regaled Ray with tales from his fishing days.

"Up in the UP, we'd catch these brook trout that'd practically melt on your tongue. Secret was cooking 'em with the head still on—kept all the flavor locked in."

Ray nodded appreciatively, slicing carrots not with the practiced stroke of a culinary student, but with the rhythm of someone who'd spent decades measuring piano songs in quarter notes.

Across the kitchen, Doris frowned at her rice pot, dipping in a small spoon and bringing it to her lips.

"This is serviceable—if you don't mind bland," she declared, reaching for her spice pouch. "Needs more than salt, though, but what ..."

Walter stood nearby adding tomato chunks and garlic to the pasta sauce. He hummed something that sounded like an old hymn, his voice blending with the kitchen's symphony.

"Lemon tree, very pretty," Merry suddenly sang out, her voice clear and bright as she pressed dough into the lemon bar pan. "and the lemon flower is sweet ..."

The melody bounced off the tile walls, and soon Ray joined in with a harmonizing bass line.

A young server poked his head through the swinging doors, inhaling deeply. "It smells like home in here," he said, grinning before disappearing back to the dining room.

Esther's heart swelled. This was what she'd meant all along—not artistry, but atmosphere.

She glanced at Diego. He stood ramrod straight at his station, tweezers in hand, delicately adjusting the arrangement on his plates. His focus never wavered, his expression never softened. A wall of professionalism surrounded him like an invisible fortress. The plate resembled something from those fancy cooking competitions on TV, not a family dinner.

Diego stepped back, tilting his head to assess his creation from different angles. He dipped a small spoon into the elements, tasting with closed eyes. A slight nod confirmed his satisfaction. It was technically flawless—Esther could see that much even from across the kitchen.

But something changed in Diego's expression as his gaze drifted toward the rest of the kitchen. His perfect dish sat isolated on its pristine counter while all around him, life happened. Carl's stew bubbled richly, slightly spilling over the edges of the pot. Doris arranged rice in earthenware bowls, not with tweezers, but with loving hands. Merry and Ray worked side by side on a cobbler, their harmonizing as sweet as the dessert itself.

Diego set down his tweezers. The motion was small but deliberate, like putting down a burden he'd carried too long. He stepped away from his station, leaving his masterpiece behind.

Esther pretended not to notice as he moved toward Doris, who was frantically searching through her spice pouch.

"I can't find my cardamom," Doris muttered, fingers moving anxiously.

"Try this," Diego said quietly, reaching into his own collection and offering her a small jar. "It's freshly ground."

Doris accepted with a nod, sprinkling a pinch into her rice mixture.

Diego drifted to Carl's station next. Without a word, he picked up the wooden spoon and gave the stew a single, gentle stir. Carl watched him with narrowed eyes.

"You gonna judge, or taste?" Carl challenged, pushing a tasting spoon toward him.

Diego hesitated only a moment before accepting. He took a careful spoonful, letting the rich broth fill his mouth. Something softened in his face.

"It's good," he admitted.

Carl's mouth quirked upward. "Of course it is ... it's stew."

The simple exchange broke something open in the room. Ray offered Diego a taste of his cornbread. Merry insisted he try her lemon curd. Walter, even stoic Walter, offered the tasting spoon of his pasta sauce.

Esther noticed how Diego didn't critique or correct. Instead, he asked questions. "What makes the cornbread so moist?" "How long have you been making this recipe?" When he did make suggestions, they were gentle, curious: "Have you ever tried adding a touch of rosemary?"

She even thought she saw a hint of a grin when he asked Carl how much chopped onion he had added to the stew, and Carl replied, "As much as it took!"

There was no dramatic transformation, no grand speech. Just a chef in a starched white coat, standing among home cooks in their worn aprons, his shoulders gradually relaxing as if setting down an invisible weight.

Esther recognized the shift in him—release. The quiet liberation that comes from realizing you don't always have to lead the orchestra to enjoy the music.

They were going to deliver this meal, and it wouldn't be the leftovers from a kitchen food-fight after all.

Service time arrived. Esther surveyed the dining hall, doubt and relief warred within her. The room glowed golden under soft lights, tables draped in simple cloth instead of the usual starched linens. Families streamed in, embracing residents with exclamations of delight.

She wiped her hands on her apron, watching as platters emerged from the kitchen. Carl's beef stew came out first, rich and fragrant, the steam carrying memories of campfires and lakeside suppers. Doris followed with her perfectly seasoned rice, explaining to a cluster of attentive guests how cardamom was the secret ingredient her mother had taught her.

"You have to toast it first," Doris instructed, her rolled sleeve revealing her pin cushion still attached to her cardigan.

Walter delivered the pasta sauce and noodles to the serving buffet with the assistance of the push cart and several servers. Ray ensured there was butter within easy reach of the cornbread.

Merry carried out a tray of lemon bars, her voice lifting in a gentle lounge tune that made heads turn and smile.

From across the room, Esther caught Mr. Carter's eye. The director stood perfectly still at the edge of the celebration, his usual composed expression replaced by something like wonder. He nodded to her, a small admission that spoke volumes.

This wasn't institutional dining. This was communion.

Esther watched Diego slip back into the kitchen, away from the growing warmth of the dining hall. The families' delighted chatter faded behind the swinging doors as she followed him, keeping a respectful distance.

He moved with purpose toward his station where his masterpiece sat untouched—the deconstructed shepherd's pie with its perfect spirals of potato purée, the precise dots of demi-glace, the architectural arrangement of vegetables. All that work, all that painstaking effort. All that loneliness.

Diego stood before it, shoulders rigid beneath his pristine white coat. Esther held her breath. She'd seen that look before—the battle between pride and belonging playing out in the set of his jaw, the slight tremble of his fingers.

He picked up the plate, turning it slowly in his hands. The lighting caught each element exactly as he'd designed it. A perfect dish. A perfect performance.

Esther expected anger, perhaps a flash of resentment. Instead, Diego's expression softened into something like peace. Without ceremony, he slid the plate into the cooler, closing the door with a gentle click.

He removed his phone from his pocket, placed it on a shelf, and reached for a ladle. Moving to the pot of Carl's stew, he began filling bowls with steady hands, arranging them on a serving tray.

Esther felt her throat tighten. This wasn't surrender—his movements held none of the stiffness of defeat. This was something rarer, something harder won. He'd chosen connection over performance, nourishment over display.

She stepped forward, picking up another ladle.

"What, no tweezers for the stew? Do you have the flu now?" Esther asked.

"Turns out stew doesn't need styling. It just needs serving." Diego replied. The smile on his face was the first she had ever seen.

Gathering the last of the napkins, Esther folded them with practiced hands. The kitchen gleamed in the dimmed lights, countertops scrubbed clean, dishes stacked neatly. Through the service window, she could see a few family members lingering at tables, reluctant to leave the warmth they'd found.

She paused, noticing Diego standing at the prep counter. His posture had changed—arms folded across his chest like someone holding a precious memory. His gaze was distant, fixed on nothing in particular, his face relaxed in a way she hadn't seen before.

The kitchen felt different, as if something had been washed away beyond just the food stains and flour dust.

Esther approached Diego, her footsteps soft against the kitchen floor. Something in his expression – unguarded, thoughtful – made her pause before speaking.

"That went well," she offered, sliding a stack of recipe cards into her apron pocket.

Diego turned, the harsh overhead lights catching the exhaustion in his eyes. "It was … different. At first, I was trying to drown out all the chatter, the stories, the sharing, and just focus on plating my food perfectly. Paying attention to how a photo might look, or what lighting and angle would capture it best. But then, I was just drawn in. The dishes they were cooking didn't stand on their own, they were an extension of each person. "

"Food has memory," Esther said, wiping her hands on her apron out of habit.

"I've been missing that point recently." Diego's voice dropped. "It started that way, but somehow, things shifted. Lately, I've been cooking for likes, for validation. For my ego." He glanced toward the dining room where laughter still echoed. "You knew better. You always did."

Esther clasped and unclasped her fingers as she listened. "Just been around longer, that's all. And haven't faced the lure of fame and a following."

"What happened today was good ... very good. I want you on the team permanently. Not just for socials. Every day, every menu." He straightened, regaining some of his professional demeanor. "Would you consider it?"

"On one condition."

"Name it," he said.

"No more tweezers at breakfast," Esther said with a small smile. "And the residents get a say in the menu. That's two conditions, I suppose."

"Deal, and deal," he said.

"So what's for breakfast tomorrow?" she asked, running her finger along the edge of the counter. "Something without tweezers—it's in my contract."

Diego's face relaxed into an easy grin she hadn't seen before. "I was thinking of going back to my college days, before culinary school. Cinnamon French toast. Thick-cut bread, real maple syrup."

"No foam?" Esther raised an eyebrow.

"No foam," Diego promised. "Unless whipped cream counts. The kind that melts into puddles and makes you lick your fingers."

Blessed Are
The Weary

*D*ana had successfully deluded herself, but now, that comfortable little lie was slipping.

She sat in the pew next to Cheryl.

Samantha sat with Callie, Amber, and the other youth group kids, just like always.

But Ron's "business trip" was becoming excessively, unbelievably, long. Dana suspected she was the topic of every whispered conversation taking place at New Life these days; that each glance or smile masked pity and judgement.

Cheryl knew the truth, of course. So did Pastor Reed. It wasn't business that was keeping Ron away, it was discontent, disillusionment, and most recently a much younger blonde.

Cheryl, as if sensing her thoughts, reached over and squeezed her hand, mouthing the words: "You will rise." Cheryl's go-to encouragement lately.

Dana tried to follow Pastor Reed's sermon on

1 Corinthians 15:58. When he read the verse, "Therefore, my beloved brothers, be steadfast, immovable, always abounding in the work of the Lord, knowing that in the Lord your labor is not in vain," she wondered if he'd picked it with her in mind; she was nothing if not abounding in the work of the Lord. That had been her and Ron's life for the past 10 or 15 years.

They worked at their jobs, and then worked again for the Lord. They were a great team, right up until Ron announced he was done and walked out.

"Hold tight," Pastor Reed said in that slightly louder tone that Dana suspected was meant to re-engage those whose thoughts had wandered.

Guilty.

She tried to listen, to hear what she needed to hear, but every word rang hollow, unhelpful. Now, of all times, she really needed that anchor of faith, but she kept drifting.

She and Ron had invested so much here—time, money, themselves. They had worked in the nursery, then in Sunday School when Sam was young. They had volunteered for countless adult and teen activities. They had given faithfully of their time, and money.

She stared at the scenes in the stained-glass windows they helped fund. Today, the brightly colored glass that usually inspired her cast an ugly, purple bruise across the sanctuary.

The praise team joined Pastor Reed on the

platform, and they began to sing the closing song. Dana felt no joy or comfort in the words she sang; felt no inspiration from the closing prayer. She seemed to feel very little, these days.

The congregation filed out into the vestibule, and eventually the parking lot. Dana waited for Samantha to say goodbye to her friends.

"Oh honey, this too shall pass." Cheryl offered with a light hug. "Hosting the Women's Ministry planning dinner this week will do you good. It will give you something to take your mind off things."

Dana nodded. Cheryl could at least call her situation 'things'. Nobody else that she had invested the last fifteen years living life with bothered to call it anything. They all avoided the topic like the plague. Have a good week, or take care were all that they managed. They had to know; there's no way they didn't know. The only thing that spread faster than blessings in a church was gossip.

Sam finally wrapped things up, and joined her and Cheryl in the parking lot.

Dana took a deep breath, ready to put her Sunday obligations behind her. "Thanks for your support, Cheryl. I don't know where I'd be without you."

"Anything you need, just call me," Cheryl said. With one final squeeze, she headed for her car.

Dana and Sam packed into her dark blue Pacifica. She had successfully navigated another Sunday without Ron. Without incident. Without much feeling at all.

"You know she's dressing to please a man, not to please the Lord when she wears something like that." Cheryl said. She was placing the sandwich quarters neatly on a serving plate.

Samantha paused at the kitchen doorway. "Mom, I'm heading over to Amanda's house. We're going to study together while you're having your meeting tonight."

"Make sure some studying actually goes on, okay? And we should be wrapping up by nine o'clock. Don't be too late." Dana looked up from mixing the broccoli salad and gave Sam a smile. She was being a trooper through all this upheaval. Dana knew it had to be eating her up too, but she had that teenage resilience going for her. Oh, to be a teen again.

"What's next, chef?" Cheryl asked. She slid the sandwich tray into the fridge among the other prepped items. "You're a master at this, by the way."

"Just using my gifts." Dana couldn't muster much enthusiasm for the thought, however. Sandwiches and salads. Nothing amazing. The kitchen tonight was simply functional, no sounds of joyful cooking, no smells of an amazing dinner.

"I feel for you, but you are handling things amazingly. What doesn't kill you makes you stronger, right?" Cheryl took the utensils she had been using to the sink and began washing.

"I think we're good for dinner, anyway." Dana mentally went back through her food list. Yep, all set.

She sat on one of the stools at the island.

"I don't feel like I'm handling things amazingly, and I'm not so sure this won't kill me either. This is something I never expected. It's not something I have any idea how to handle and I just don't know where to turn."

Saying it out loud felt strangely good. Since Ron had walked out, she'd been doing everything she could just to keep her crap together. Finally admitting she felt like her life was unraveling, offered a bit of relief.

"You know, Honey, he will never leave you or forsake you." Cherly offered, joining her on the other stool.

Dana waited, hoping Cheryl might have some other insight … something with a little more teeth for the moment.

The silence stretched.

She felt Cheryl would rather tread close to the surface but the moment felt cathartic; Dana didn't relent. "I just need something more, right now, than—"

The doorbell rang.

"I'll get that." Cheryl practically ran for the door. Before passing from the kitchen, she turned back, saying, "You take a minute to get yourself together. You don't want anyone to see you like this."

Nope, I wouldn't want that.

Dana sat in one of the armchairs in the empty greatroom. Faces from pictures of better times stared at her from the mantle.

The Women's Ministry group had expertly steered the evening towards compliments about the food, idle chatter about the weather, cleanliness of her house—next to Godliness, and a plethora of activities Dana could assist in planning and coordinating. At Cheryl's urging, they all helped clean up the kitchen, ensured the dishes were put away, and left as quickly as politely possible, Cheryl included.

Sam had come home on time, confirmed she had, indeed, studied. She confessed it hadn't been as long as it should have been, and headed to her room for a little more chemistry review before bed.

Dana glanced down the row of pictures again, feeling their mocking, accusing, lying stares.

On her way out, Cheryl had actually said: "You did good tonight, Honey. You really kept it together. Having this ministry to look forward to will give you focus."

Dana felt a scream building inside. If Sam weren't upstairs, she would let it out like the whistle of steam rushing off a pressure cooker. She could imagine the relief of opening her voice to the shame, and hatred, and betrayal, and loneliness she had felt over the last few weeks. It would do absolutely no good, except she knew the release would feel amazing.

Instead, she went to the pantry and retrieved a black garbage bag. She returned and cleared the mantle of every picture that didn't have Sam in it. Her wedding photo with Ron was the first, dropped roughly into the bag.

A photo from their honeymoon went next. There was a satisfying shatter as it joined the wedding photo in the bag.

Ten year anniversary. Solo vacation at the beach. And finally, the photo of them receiving the Distinguished Service Award from New Light Fellowship two years ago.

Dana surveyed the more spacious mantle.

Much better.

She carried the bag to the master bathroom.

Razor, shaving cream, toothbrush, and cologne all joined the photos. More satisfying breakage as they struck the frames.

Ron's bedside table was next—only the lamp was spared.

Dana pulled the ties on the garbage bag and heaved it satisfyingly into the floor of Ron's closet in the bedroom; she didn't have the heart to take it to the trash—not yet.

Work the next day passed with typical monotony, and Sam was home already when she arrived. Her daughter had the table set with leftovers from last night, and had added homemade mac and cheese to the menu as well.

"You're amazing," Dana said, giving her daughter a long hug. "I think we could both use a little comfort food."

"That's exactly what I thought," Samantha said. "I am amazing."

They both laughed, holding each other tighter. It was the first real laugh in a long time. Dana could feel her shoulders relax, some of the stress of the day, or maybe week, sliding away.

As they ate, Sam shared bits about her day. The chemistry exam went better than expected. School lunch wasn't as bad as usual. Amber and Callie were so excited about starting drivers training soon; Sam confided that she was still a little nervous about it herself.

"Do we have anything going Thursday night?" Sam asked.

"Not that I know of, what's up?"

Dana could sense her daughter's nervous excitement, and wondered if she wanted to ask about inviting a boy to dinner–she'd been talking a lot about Tommy Johnson lately.

"Ms. Nolan, our art teacher, is hosting an art showcase at the community center Thursday night. She's going to be including some pieces from kids at school, and one of them is mine."

"Sam, that's amazing!" She had always loved art classes in school. Dana, like any proud parent, had been supportive, but she'd never thought it was something that Sam excelled at. "Tell me about your piece. What is it?"

"It's a painting of some fruit," Sam said. "Ms. Nolan said it is raw, and honest."

"Raw and honest fruit—how could I miss that." Dana said.

Ms. Nolan had moved to town several years ago when the old art teacher retired. She had opened a small shop in town that Dana and Ron had visited, and Dana remembered she seemed a bit … atypical for the community.

On that visit, she'd been wearing a black t-shirt and loose coverall jeans both blotched with a variety of paint colors. Her hair, then, had been cut very short, and tinted towards blue.

The art in the shop was a strange mix of curiosities, far from anything Dana would choose to hang on her walls.

"I'm sure she has quite an eye for beauty," Ron had teased after the visit. "We probably share the same taste in brunettes."

Remembering that comment made Dana's heart beat faster.

"You okay, Mom?" Sam asked.

"Sorry, lost in the past for a minute," Dana said. She scooped another helping of mac and cheese, then tried to get her thoughts back on track.

"Are other kids showing pieces as well?"

Samantha began providing details of the other student art to be included, but Dana's mind wandered.

Ms. Nolan–wasn't her first name Barbara? Ron and Dana had invited her to church on that first visit, but she'd politely declined. In her first year of teaching, the Women's Ministry council had several discussions about the wisdom of someone like that guiding the minds of the town's young women. At the time, Dana thought they were overreacting.

And on the several occasions when their paths had crossed since, the woman had come across ... well, just kookie. Strange. Definitely what Ron would refer to as "the artsy type."

I can go, take a quick peek at Samantha's painting, and politely retreat.

"Mom, did you hear a word I said?" Sam asked, carrying plates to the sink.

"Sorry. I was ... thinking." Dana joined with the light clean-up. "What were you saying?"

"I said I can't wait for you to meet Ms. Nolan. I've talked to her some ... you know, about Dad, and stuff. She's helped me a lot."

Dana was horrified. Her daughter had been airing the family's dirty laundry with her teacher! She did her best not to let the shock show. What was Sam thinking? Especially that teacher.

It was bad enough that people at church were talking behind her back, but a complete stranger.

She took a deep, steadying breath. Let it go for now. On Thursday, I'll tell Sam I don't feel well. She'll be disappointed, but she'll get over it. I can see the picture when she brings it home.

"I'm heading up to study a bit, and I'm working on another sketch." Sam slid the last plate into the dishwasher and closed it. "I'm glad you're coming on Thursday. I can't wait for you to see my picture, but I really can't wait for you to talk with Ms. Nolan. You know, she teaches art classes on Tuesday evenings, maybe we could go to one together."

"I'll think about it," Dana replied.

Not a chance.

Sam left the kitchen and Dana called after her: "Thanks again for dinner."

There was no way Dana had any time to spare for an art class with a busybody who thought they knew anything about her situation, or how to cope with it.

Dana had fully intended to back out, but Sam was so excited. For a moment, the battle had raged in Dana's head, but in the end mother's love had won over fear, and they'd packed into the car and headed to the community center for the art showcase.

The large room screamed municipal utility featuring off white block walls, fluorescent lighting, and a low-pile olive green carpeting in replaceable squares.

Throughout the room, makeshift walls had been erected with dark colored curtains strung between posts, providing isolated backdrops for showcasing the works. There were paintings on easels, tables containing pottery or homemade jewelry, a variety of large and small sculptures–some clay, some metal, and one replica of a small car made completely from old license plates.

The crowd was larger than Dana had expected, and seemed to represent a diverse cross section of town. While she didn't see anyone she knew from church, she did recognize the clerk from the grocery, the man who often wiped down the cars at the carwash, a man who she was pretty sure regularly begged for handouts near the local Kroger, and a lunch lady from the highschool–but maybe she worked at the nursing home now, didn't she?

Surveying the odd collection of both art and people, she spotted Barbara Nolan walking her way. She was wearing what looked like motorcycle boots, jeans with out-of-fashion rips, and a baggy black and red flannel shirt. Her hair was still short, but she was sporting a dark red tint these days.

Dana could tell she'd seen them, and was headed over, but along the way, she paused to shake hands or greet the visitors she came across.

She passed an elderly gentleman with a walker who was struggling to place a large painting of a chihuahua onto an easel. The painting listed sideways, but Ms. Nolan steadied it with one hand and the gentleman with the other. They laughed at some shared comment and Barbara gave him a quick hug before moving on.

"Thought that dog was going for a run," she said as she greeted Sam and Dana.

"Hi, Ms. Nolan," Sam said. "This is my mom."

"Pleased to meet you," Barbara said, exchanging a quick handshake. Her hands were calloused and rough. Manly.

"Likewise. I'm sorry if Samantha has been burdening you with our personal a-affairs," Dana stumbled at the poor word choice; she had intended to completely ignore the subject, but it just came out.

"Mom!"

Ms. Nolan gave Samantha a slight nod and half smile. "Art reflects life, and sometimes both can be messy, right Samantha?"

"Right ... like now." Samantha said, glaring at her mother.

"Thank you so much for coming tonight. I'm sure you're excited to see Samantha's painting. She's really done a great job with it. All the student pieces are over here."

Ms. Nolan led them on a zig-zag route past pastel watercolor landscapes, a collection of brightly colored flower paintings, and a man-sized copper and brass robot.

She slowed when she arrived at a set of five

easels showing still life paintings of fruit. In each portrait, the arrangement and variety of the fruit was different. Ms. Nolan directed them to the middle portrait and stopped.

Dana took in the image. The fruit was depicted in vivid detail, a banana, an orange, and an apple. In the pictures on either side, the fruit may not have been drawn quite as well, but in each of them it was brightly colored and appeared fresh and firm. Inviting.

In this picture–Sam's picture–the fruit was wonderfully rendered, but showing blemishes and signs of decay. The banana was browning, the apple was shriveling with a large rotten spot near the bottom, and the orange was collapsing in on itself with spots of grey mould.

"Well, I can tell exactly what it is ..." Dana stifled her visceral reaction to the image. "I ... it ..."

Barbara saved her. "Samantha found this exercise a productive outlet to deal with some of her recent feelings. Her work here is excellent. She has used the lighting and shadows to convey the feeling of the piece, and her brushwork is just wonderful."

All Dana saw was rotting fruit; was that how Sam felt about what was going on? Was Ms. Nolan going to use this as a way to criticize Dana's handling of the situation? Of her parenting? Dana could feel her defenses rising.

"I'm sorry, but I need to make the rounds with the other visitors. I'll leave you to explore the rest of the show together." Apparently Dana's worry had been for nothing. "If you have any questions, please find me, though. I'd be more than happy to chat. And between us, I understand what you are going through. If you ever feel it would be helpful to talk to someone who's walked in your shoes, I'd be more than happy to chat about that too. Any time."

Ms. Nolan turned and walked back towards the entrance, pausing at several booths along the way to offer a quick word.

Dana was flabbergasted. This was not at all what she had expected.

"Isn't she great, Mom?" Sam whispered.

"She was certainly nice enough," Dana admitted.

She turned back to Sam's painting. The longer she stared at it, the more the condition of the fruit felt—right. She put her arm around Sam's shoulder, pulled her close, and planted a light kiss on her temple.

"At first, this really disturbed me ... but somehow, now it doesn't."

"I know, right? I tried painting it like the other kids, perfect and pleasing, but that never worked ... it never came out right."

Sam launched into the details of her failed attempts, and color choices, and brush stroke approaches. She also shared how Ms. Nolan had encouraged her to allow her feelings to flow into the painting. How she'd listened quietly when Sam had just needed to vent. How she hadn't judged, just supported. Sam didn't use those words, exactly, but that was the message Dana heard. It was the most she had heard Sam share in a while, and her enthusiasm for painting, and Ms. Nolan, was infectious.

They walked around together to explore the other exhibits. Some they loved, some they hated, and some were just confusing. There was even a whole table of pictures of plated food. They looked gorgeous, but Dana didn't imagine they tasted as good as they looked.

Occasionally, she would spot Barbara engaged in conversation with guests, pointing to various pieces, smiling and laughing. The way she interacted with the visitors; the way she had offered support to Dana, reflected an amazing grace. Dana felt slightly ashamed of her preconceptions.

When they had completed the rounds and were heading to the door, Sam asked: "So, what do you think about us trying those art classes together?"

"I'll think about it," she said. This time, she really meant it.

When Dana arrived at the Sunny Side Cafe, Cheryl already had a table for them. She waved enthusiastically when she saw Dana enter. Dana replied with an obligatory half wave.

"Oh, there you are Honey. It's so good to see you." Cheryl's zeal never seemed to wane. "How are you? The Women's Ministry dinner the other night was wonderful, by the way."

She knew Cheryl meant well, but already, Dana was feeling drained. She'd really just wanted to stay at home today, hide away in the house, and sulk privately.

The diner, which she normally considered cute and charming, felt fake today. Probably it was a reflection of her mood, but today the plastic checkered tablecloths topped with mason jars of fake flowers and the sappy inspirational slogans on the walls made her stomach churn.

"I'm doing okay," she said. She wasn't, but she knew taking the conversation any deeper would trigger a barrage of platitudes from Cheryl.

"You're just so strong. You got this. So ... I was thinking that we should organize a Women's Weekend. I think it would be a great opportunity ..." And she was off.

She shared her ideas of what a perfect Women's Weekend would look like, and the jobs that Dana would have to make it happen, only pausing to order coffee and breakfast.

Dana tried to listen, but she didn't have it in her today. She looked around at the other patrons. None seemed as affected by the decor as she was. A husband, wife, and young daughter enjoyed pancakes, the young girls' done up with smiley faces. An older couple chatting over coffee.

At a table in the back, two women and a man were carrying on an animated conversation. Their plates were pushed away half eaten, food giving way to their energized conversation. The woman with the reddish curly hair tossed her head back in laughter. The man thumped the table and grinned, deep crow's feet framing his eyes.

Dana recognized the other woman, who snorted a laugh and rubbed tears from her. The grocery store clerk who she'd seen the other night at the art workshop. Now that she'd placed her, the others seemed familiar too, maybe they had been at the community center as well.

"Have you heard a word I've said?" Cheryl drew her back to their conversation. "I know I talk too much, sometimes. My mama used to say: 'You don't stop for a minute, do ya?' I just don't know what would happen if I stopped; I might not like being alone with myself in the quiet."

Cheryl folded her hands in her lap and dropped her eyes like a child who had just been scolded.

"I'm sorry, Cheryl. My head is all over the place these days. Yes, I think those are all great ideas."It really sounded awful, but she couldn't say that, especially now.

Cheryl's exuberance came back in full force.

"Atta girl! And it will do you good. Idle hands are the Devil's workshop, after all." Cheryl drank the last sip of her coffee, and waved the cup slightly towards the waitress for a refill.

Breakfast arrived.

Dana struggled to pay closer attention to what Cheryl was saying.

The food tasted bland, and Dana nearly spilled her coffee when Cheryl suggested fruit of the spirit cupcakes at the retreat–each flavored and decorated—as if joy and buttercream were the same thing.

At the art workshop, Barbara had been content to offer support. Cheryl wanted to fill every moment with activity. Barbara had taken the time to lend a hand when needed, or offer an encouraging word. With Cheryl, it was hard to get a word in edgewise.

Laughter bubbled over again from the table in the corner. Several other patrons turned, smiling at the ruckus. Dana found herself wondering if they were talking about their latest creative project, sampling a new recipe for guacamole, or the result of washing a load of clothes in the wrong water temperature.

"I'm so glad we got to connect, today, and I'm so glad you're willing to help organize the Women's Weekend."

Dana didn't remember agreeing to do it, but often that was an overlooked detail for Cheryl.

"And I got you something." She reached into her oversized purse and handed Dana a small wrapped rectangle.

Dana unwrapped a framed sign that read: "Blessed are the Strong." It looked like it would be right at home on one of the diner's walls.

"I don't know what to say," was as much as Dana could muster.

"You don't need to say a thing, Honey." Cheryl came around the table and gave Dana a hug. "Sorry, but I gotta scoot. I'll see you at service tomorrow. Call if you need anything. And this is on me."

Dana watched Cheryl pay the bill, give one more wave, and exit the diner. The cheerful chime of the bell over the door was annoying.

She looked at the sign once more and thought, *What happened to: "Come to me all who are weary and heavy laden, and I will give you rest?"*

The text arrived on Monday evening. It read: Sam says you might join tomorrow night. Please do. When my husband and I split, I didn't have the support I needed. Don't want anyone to ever feel that way. Barbara.

At first, she was shocked that Ms. Nolan had her phone number, but to Sam, texting was the only form of communication.

She was touched by the offer, and Barbara's frankness about everything. She longed for one of her friends to be this open, but even Cheryl was quick to close down any meaningful discussion.

For a moment, she had the impulse to call Barbara back, and spill everything out on the phone like she did with her girlfriends when she was a teenager.

In the end, she simply replied: "Thanks. Still considering."

Dana put the last dish away and shut the cupboard. She looked around the kitchen searching for more work. Neat as a pin.

She sighed.

Sam's text had said, "Art class tonight. Lmk if you're coming."

She retrieved a black plastic garbage bag from the pantry.

The image of Barbara going from person to person at the art showcase came to mind. Dana recalled her offer "If you ever feel it would be helpful to talk to someone who's walked in your shoes ..."

She went to the bedroom, opened Ron's closet, and stared at the clothes.

Cheryl's platitudes came to mind.

Idle hands are the Devil's Workshop.

The "Blessed are the Strong" framed photo that was still in the backseat of her car.

She couldn't shake the isolation she had felt for weeks among the people who were supposed to be her closest friends and support group.

She removed several shirts and dumped them into the garbage bag, hangers and all.

She thought of Samantha's picture of rotting fruit and heard Barbara say, "Samantha found this exercise a productive outlet to deal with some of her recent feelings."

"I was struggling so much more until I got my feelings out on the canvas," Sam had said that night.

Dana added Ron's dress pants to the garbage bag.

Life was unravelling, and she needed help; what she was doing wasn't working.

As she reached for more clothes, she noticed her hand was trembling. The closet blurred, as Dana teared up.

"How could you do this to me?"

She dropped the bag, unsure exactly who the comment was directed at, and wiped her eyes.

She remembered the trio at the cafe, sharing such joy.

Come to me, all who are weary ...

Maybe I've had everything all wrong. Maybe I've been doing all the right things, but for the wrong reasons. Maybe grace can look different than what I've always known.

She took a deep steadying breath, wiped her eyes again, left the bag on the floor, and headed to grab her purse and car keys.

The community center parking lot had more cars than Dana expected.

She sat and gripped the steering wheel too

tightly, her knuckles turning white.

She thought of the Women's Ministry group's judgement of people like Barbara.

And how could she expect a secular art class, and the people who would be here, to be a better support group than her church family? It might have worked for Sam, but she was young and impressionable.

Maybe I've been an awful mother. I haven't been careful enough about who my daughter has been associating with.

Dana considered that Sam seemed to be coping with the situation pretty well, though.

It's just a couple of hours to try my hand at painting.

But she knew that was a lie too. What she most wanted was to sit with Barbara and spill everything.

To open up to someone.

To explain how trapped she felt. How powerless.

To scream that she'd like to kill that bastard for doing this to her!

She took a deep, shuddering breath.

Wouldn't that set the Women's Ministry group a buzz! She couldn't hold back a sharp laugh at the thought.

Forget it all. Go in here, hear about how to properly hold a brush. Dab some paint. Connect with Barbara, and see if she really did understand what it was like to walk in Dana's shoes.

She gave another barking laugh as she pictured Ms. Nolan in coveralls and Dana's favorite yellow Sunday heels.

Cheryl would get up on her high horse and ride it for hours. She would say, "Oh Honey, you need prayer."

She would have that condescending arch to her eyebrows when Dana told her where she'd spent her Tuesday night. As if it was a casino or strip club.

Dana closed her eyes and pushed her head back against the headrest as hard as she could. She tightened every muscle in her body, then released the tension.

It felt as if this moment was deciding her fate for the rest of her life.

It was just a stupid art class. A considerate offer of help.

But Dana couldn't shake the fact that it seemed like she would be turning her back on everything she had been taught about what is sacred and proper. And she could just hear Cheryl whispering to the other Women's Ministry ladies, "Did you hear about Dana, spending all that time with Barbara Nolan and those people. It's no wonder Ron left her."

Church people minister to people like Barbara; they don't join them.

Church people set a good example. There are certain associations that good, proper church people avoid. If your faith isn't strong enough to get you through a tough time, what kind of faith is it?

And faith without works is dead.

Dana reached into the backseat and retrieved the framed photo Cheryl had given her.

Blessed are the Strong.

"This too shall pass," she said.

She grabbed her phone and shot a quick text to Sam: "Sorry, I don't think art class is for me. But you enjoy it!"

She read it over, deleted the last line, and clicked send.

Dana carefully placed the framed slogan on the mantle.

She went to the bedroom, stuffed more of Ron's clothes into the black garbage bag. Retrieved the other bag with the frames from the bottom of the closet, and dumped both into the garbage can in the garage.

Finally, she retrieved her notebook and pen, and returned to the living room. As she walked past, she adjusted the angle of the Blessed are the Strong picture slightly, then sat with her legs curled up on the couch.

She titled the page: Women's Weekend Planning, and divided it into three columns: Ministry Session, Fun and Games, and Food.The first two, she subdivided into Time, Leader, and

Details.

She divided the food column into Person and Item, then entered Dana - Fruits of the Spirit Cupcakes.

Marcy's Notebook And The Canine Conspiracy

*M**aple Creek Estates stood as a testament to suburban uniformity—twenty-seven houses with matching slate-gray roofs, evenly spaced maple trees, and lawns maintained at precisely three inches. The neighborhood hummed with the quiet rhythm of morning newspaper retrievals and evening garbage can placements. Residents exchanged cordial nods across driveways and occasional comments about the weather, but little more.*

Marcy Greenfield surveyed the street from her bay window, notebook open on her lap. Section 4, Paragraph 12 of the HOA guidelines clearly stated that holiday decorations, excepting Christmas, must be removed within five days of the holiday's conclusion. The Millers' forgotten Valentine's wreath still hung on their door—eight days after

February 14th.

"Unacceptable," she muttered, making a precise note in her Community Log Action Item list directly under the reminder to discuss moving van parking time limits and moving box disposal guidelines with the new residents in House #18.

As self-appointed guardian of neighborhood standards, Marcy took her unofficial position seriously. The elected HOA board met only twice a year, but neighborhood vigilance required daily attention. In her kitchen drawers, she retained fourteen years' worth of meeting minutes. On her bookshelf she displayed the rulebook, with tabs color-coded by violation frequency, in a place of honor, next to a portrait of her late husband Ben.

"The neighborhood has changed, Ben. It's not like it used to be."

Marcy smoothed her ruler-straight bangs and stood to prepare her morning tea. The residents might roll their eyes behind her back, but someone needed to maintain order. Without standards, chaos would reign—basketball hoops would appear in driveways, mailboxes would display unapproved colors, and before you knew it, a recreational vehicle would be parked in plain sight.

The kettle whistled. Marcy poured water over her chamomile tea bag—steeping for exactly three minutes. She retrieved her tea biscuits from their spot on the shelf when movement on the front porch caught her eye.

A dog. Not just any dog, but an enormous, shaggy creature with mismatched patches of sandy gold and cream fur and inquisitive pumpkin colored eyes. No collar. No leash. No human in sight.

Marcy frowned. Section 7, Paragraph 3: All pets must be leashed when outside the owner's property.

The dog tilted his head, regarding her through the window with an expression that seemed oddly ... amused.

"Shoo," Marcy mouthed through the glass making a move-along motion with her free hand.

The dog remained seated, tail sweeping a semicircle across her welcome mat.

Marcy opened her front door a cautious three inches. "For the record, you're in violation of at least two HOA guidelines."

The dog's tail wagged faster.

She peered at his neck. "No identification whatsoever. As per Section—"

The dog yawned, displaying an impressive set of teeth.

"You need to move along. Go back to wherever you came from. You have no business here. I have animal control on speed dial, and they are aware we require prompt response to strays."

The dog tilted his head sideways again, as if considering her words, then stretched out across the welcome mat.

A new plan occurred to her. She flipped a

tea biscuit through the crack. It landed near the dog's massive front paws. With surprising gentleness, he retrieved the biscuit and regarded her, crunching contentedly.

"There. Now move along out of this neighborhood." Marcy gave the door a slight nudge to close it and turned, intent on retrieving her notebook to log the incident.

The dog seized the opportunity, bumped the door with its nose, and slipped past her legs into the house.

"Absolutely not. Exit immediately!" She tapped her foot against the hardwood, pointing to the open door.

The dog circled her living room, sniffing with methodical interest. He paused to briefly examine Marcy's house slippers, then hopped onto the couch. Turning once, he settled with his head on the armrest.

"This ... this is trespassing." Marcy reached for her Community Log. "I'll need to document this violation too. Now get out."

The dog sprang from the couch, snatched one of her slippers in his mouth, and darted for the door.

"Drop that this instant." Too late, he was out the door and off the porch.

Halfway up the walk, the dog paused to look back, eyes twinkling with mischief, then turned and loped down the sidewalk and through her hedge, the blue slipper bobbing in his mouth.

"Stop. That's personal property." She waited.

When it was clear the dog had no intention of returning, Marcy closed the door, snapped the lock in place with disgust, then settled at her kitchen table, flipping to a fresh page in her Community Log. This required a new section entirely. She labeled it in her precise handwriting: "UNIDENTIFIED CANINE VIOLATIONS."

"Subject: Large dog, no collar, sandy-gold fur with cream patches," she wrote, pressing her pen into the paper with such force it nearly tore. "First incident: February 22nd, 9:17 AM. Trespassing and theft of personal property (one blue house slipper, left foot)."

She underlined "theft" twice.

Who allowed their pet to wander freely, entering homes and stealing possessions? Thoughts racing, Marcy tapped her pen against her palm.

"Action plan," she continued writing. "1) Canvas neighborhood to identify owner. 2) Document all violations with photographic evidence if possible. 3) Present findings at emergency HOA meeting."

Marcy nodded to herself. She would start with the Hendersons, then the Patels. Someone had to know something about this four-legged menace. By week's end, she would restore order to Maple Creek Estates.

Claire, glancing out her front window, spotted Marcy's rigid posture and militaristic strides. The neighborhood's self-appointed rule enforcer marched up her walkway with that dreaded community log tucked under her arm. Claire closed her laptop, muting her corporate conference call mid-sentence. This interruption might actually be the most interesting part of her day.

She opened the door before Marcy could knock.

"Claire! I'm conducting an investigation regarding an unauthorized canine presence in our community." Marcy tapped the clipboard with the pen, punctuating each word.

Claire leaned against the doorframe. "You mean the friendly mutt that's been making rounds? The one who's currently the most exciting thing to happen in Maple Creek since the Wilsons' garden gnome collection mysteriously rearranged itself to spell 'HELP'?"

"This is a serious matter." Marcy huffed. "The Hendersons reported that this animal absconded with Mr. Henderson's porch flag—the new one that is within the HOA size limits on such displays—and left behind a pinecone. A pinecone! From a species of pine that I believe isn't native to our landscaping plan."

Claire pushed her designer glasses up with her middle finger. "Fascinating evidence."

"And the Patels discovered their garden trowel

missing yesterday morning. In its place was"—
Marcy consulted her notes—"half of a tennis ball.
Mrs. Patel claims it wasn't there the previous
evening. And to top it off, the brute forced his way
into my home, rummaged through my personal
belongings, and made off with one of my house
slippers!"

"Quite the criminal mastermind." Claire
paused, savoring the moment. "As it happens, I had
my own encounter with our four-legged friend
yesterday." She left Marcy standing on the porch,
returning a moment later with a blue slipper. "I
believe this belongs to you?"

Marcy gasped, snatching the slipper as Claire
offered it. "My Ralph Lauren!"

"Your furry culprit delivered it personally. Sat
right there on my porch slobbering all over
it, looking rather pleased with himself." Claire
crossed her arms. "Look, he's just a neighborhood
dog having some fun. The slipper is back with its
rightful owner. Maybe a little soggy, but no real
harm done. Case closed, right?"

"Absolutely not. I've delayed other important
enforcement duties, like clarifying moving truck
parking protocol, because of this dog! This
represents a clear violation of Section 7,
Paragraphs 3 through 8 regarding unrestrained
animals. I've already documented seven
infractions."

Claire's eyebrow arched. This woman needed
a hobby that didn't involve terrorizing innocent

dogs ... or neighbors. If Marcy wanted a story, Claire would give her one.

"Well, if you must know the whole truth ..." Claire lowered her voice dramatically. "When I found him with your slipper, I noticed something ... unusual."

"Unusual how?" Marcy leaned forward, pen poised.

"He was arranging small objects in a pattern. Your slipper, a bottle cap, and three perfectly aligned pebbles. When I approached, he looked me directly in the eye and barked—three short barks, three long ones, and three short again."

"You expect me to believe the dog is using Morse code?"

"Precisely. S.O.S." Claire pushed on. "Then, leaving the slipper, he swiped my Tri-County Root Canal Symposium stress ball from the end table and took off toward the road like a shot. But here's the strange part—I swear I saw him pull something from behind a bush that looked suspiciously like a small notebook."

Marcy's pen hovered ... "A notebook?"

"Similar to yours, actually. Though considerably more weathered." Claire paused. "But it's all probably nothing. Just a friendly neighborhood dog with excellent taste in footwear relieving stress."

Claire watched as Marcy's expression transformed from skepticism to intense fascination. The woman was actually buying this ridiculous story.

"A notebook?" Marcy's voice dropped to a conspiratorial whisper. "This confirms my suspicions. We're not dealing with an ordinary dog. He's up to no good. Disrupting things. Making a nuisance of himself."

Claire bit the inside of her cheek to keep from laughing. "Exactly ... a nuisance. But not just a nuisance. If everything you have documented is true, he's downright felonious! That would explain the organized theft pattern. He's sowing seeds of discontent in the neighborhood! It's a good thing we have you keeping tabs on him."

Marcy's pen flew across her community log. "We can't take this behavior lightly. We really should track his every movement."

"You're right. You should. Do you know who might have more information?" Claire suggested, already picturing the chaos about to unfold. "Jeremy Dawson. I saw him photographing the dog yesterday. Said something about unusual markings on its chest that looked like 'microtech.'"

Marcy glanced in the direction of Jeremy's house. "The Dawson boy? Unacceptable that he's withholding evidence! I'll speak with him immediately."

Claire suppressed a smile as Marcy marched off, community log clutched to her chest. Jeremy, with his flair for the dramatic and his fondness for superhero conspiracies, would take this ball and run with it spectacularly. The neighborhood was about to get far more interesting.

Jeremy slumped deeper into the beanbag chair, thumbs flying across his controller. Landing a perfect combo, he grinned at the on-screen victory.

The doorbell buzzed—twice, sharp and insistent.

He dragged himself downstairs, enduring three more rings before opening the door to find Marcy Greenfield standing there, clipboard clutched to her chest like a shield.

"Jeremy Dawson," she snapped. "Claire Matthison said you've been photographing that mutt terrorizing the neighborhood. I need answers."

Jeremy fought back a grin. Claire had sent Marcy to him? Perfect.

"What dog? " Jeremy leaned forward, suddenly invested.

Marcy tapped the clipboard. "I'm sure you know full well what dog, young man." She flipped open her color-coded notebook. "I'm tracking the animal's movements and collecting evidence. There are disturbing patterns emerging."

Jeremy ran his hand over his mouth as if deep in thought over this revelation. Claire was literally epic for this. She and Jeremy had developed an unspoken alliance ever since last summer when she caught him climbing the oak tree in her yard to rescue his drone. Instead of going to his parents or reporting him to the HOA for trespassing, she simply raised an eyebrow and said, "I expect a full flight demonstration once you retrieve it."

"Patterns? Like what?" Jeremy asked, widening his eyes.

Marcy adjusted her hair with a quick, sharp movement. "The items taken and left behind appear random, but I believe this K-9 is smarter than we think and that they're coded messages." She turned her notebook toward him, revealing meticulously drawn diagrams connecting houses with red lines. "Claire suggested you might have insights into the animal's unusual behavior and microtech."

"Ah, yes, the microtech. My own investigation isn't complete, so I don't know how much of this I should share ... but, I've been watching him for weeks! That dog is literally trained in counterintelligence techniques. The way he sits? Classic surveillance posture."

Marcy's pen froze mid tap. "Surveillance?"

"I swear! He always tilts his head exactly forty-five degrees when you talk to him. That's not cute dog behavior—he's recording your voice patterns!" Jeremy joined Marcy on the porch. "And those random objects? They're not random at all."

Marcy scribbled frantically in her notebook. "Go on."

Jeremy looked over Marcy's shoulder and

noticed Claire on her porch across the street with a coffee mug in hand. When their eyes locked, she pushed her glasses up with a deliberate middle finger. The challenge was issued.

"Ms. Greenfield," Jeremy said, lowering his voice conspiratorially, "what I'm about to tell you about that dog might blow this whole neighborhood mystery wide open."

Jeremy felt the creative fire ignite in his brain. He leaned against the doorframe, dropping his voice to a dramatic whisper.

"That dog? He's not just any dog. That's a Kravchenko Receiver mix. Super rare breed. There's only like, a handful in existence. The CIA and KGB both used them during the Cold War. They can literally smell data, Ms. Greenfield."

"Smell ... data? Come on, Jeremy." Marcy's pen hovered above her notebook.

"No, really. Literally. I've been tracking him too. Those items he's taking, he's scanning them for intel." Jeremy locked eyes with Marcy, giving his best wide-eyed wonder look. She chewed her lip for a minute, then he could see the fear win as she flipped to a fresh page and started frantically scribbling more notes.

"But who would want intel about our neighborhood?"

"I've tried to make contact with him to find out, but here's the thing"—Jeremy leaned closer—"he only responds to commands in French or Eskimo. I even tried anime Japanese; no reaction."

"French? Or Eskimo?" Marcy was writing so forcefully, Jeremy felt sorry for the notebook. "But why?"

"Took me a while to figure it out too, but the only thing that fits is the annual HOA board elections," Jeremy said matter of factly. "I started seeing some internet posts related to the stuff he's been carrying around, and for sure, he's working with the Extraterrestrial Homeowners Alliance. They're trying to infiltrate and take over our HOA!"

"Extraterrestrial?" Marcy's face paled.

"I didn't believe it at first, but the evidence on the internet is legit. Think about it! They're planning to replace our HOA with their own alien governance structure." Jeremy pounded his fist into his hand. "They want to invade and abolish our current HOA completely!"

"Aliens, Jeremy? Really?" Marcy had stopped writing. Maybe he'd gone too far.

"Oh, no, not space aliens. That's silly. Everything on the web ties back to the Ohio Homeowners Alliance. They're probably looking to swoop in and reorganize everything. I hear those people in the OHA oppose guidelines for lawn signs, have no time window for garbage cans on the street—before or after pickup—and only meet every two years. Can you imagine? With all the intel that dog has provided—we're toast!"

Clutching her notebook to her chest, Marcy recoiled in horror. "I ... I ... I never even considered!

This is worse than I imagined. We need an emergency meeting. Tonight!"

"You should definitely call everyone together." Jeremy nodded solemnly. "Before it's too late."

Marcy spun on her heel, already dialing on her phone as she marched down the walkway. Jeremy watched her hurry away then glanced across the street where Claire still sat on her porch. He raised his hand in a slow, deliberate salute, grinning as she lifted her coffee mug in acknowledgment.

Marcy ran the laser pointer over the diagram a final time for emphasis before advancing to her conclusion. Her twenty-minute presentation on the "Canine Infiltrator" had included a detailed map of the neighborhood with red lines connecting each dog sighting, three blurry photographs, and a color-coded spreadsheet of "suspicious objects and their movement."

"And that concludes my evidence that we are dealing with an Ohio alien intelligence gathering French-Eskimo speaking spy dog," Marcy declared, snapping her laser pointer off with a flourish. "Questions?"

The community center fell silent. Harold Baxter, the HOA's official president, cleared his throat and rose from his chair at the head of the table. "Well now, Marcy, that was certainly ... comprehensive." Harold glanced at Claire, who was stifling a laugh, and Jeremy, whose shoulders shook with silent mirth. "Though I'm not entirely sure how you arrived at some of those conclusions. Particularly the part about the dog transmitting neighborhood secrets to the Russians."

"Ohio Homeowners Alliance, he's just Russian trained," Marcy corrected. "The evidence speaks for itself, Harold. How else do you explain the systematic redistribution of household items? It's clearly a sophisticated intelligence-gathering operation."

Harold chuckled and ran his hand through his graying, thinning hair. "Back in my day as principal, we had a therapy dog that used to steal erasers from every classroom. Turned out he just liked the smell of chalk. Simple as that."

"This is different," Marcy insisted, feeling her certainty waver slightly. "This dog has purpose."

"I'm not sure about the dog's purpose," Claire said. "But I've never seen an HOA meeting this entertaining. Usually it's just complaints about hedge heights and garbage can placement, but this has been fun!"

"I've never come to one of these before. My parents say they're a boring waste of time," Jeremy added.

His father lowered his head, closely examining his shoes, while his mother covered her mouth with her hand.

"But if it's like this every time, count me in. Uh, and I swear that dog understood what I was saying yesterday. I asked who he was working for and he played dumb perfectly!"

Mrs. Rodriguez from two streets over raised her hand. "My grandmother in Mexico would say this dog is a guardian spirit. They call them 'naguals'—protectors who bring communities together."

"That's ridiculous," Marcy started, but noticed several heads nodding. The room was engaged, animated—more lively than any HOA meeting she could remember. Usually by now, Mr. Wilson would be checking his watch and Mrs. Petrovich would be scrolling through her phone.

"You know," Harold said, leaning forward on his elbows, "whatever this dog is or isn't, we haven't talk to each other this much in the fifteen years I've lived here."

Claire smiled. "He's right. I've learned more names in the past week, chasing and returning things that the dog has left, than in the past two years combined."

Mrs. Rodriguez chimed in. "He brought me a single sock from who-knows-where, then just plopped down on my porch like he'd delivered a priceless treasure. Tail wagging the entire time. I had no idea who it belonged to, so I ended up knocking on three doors that night—I met two neighbors I'd never spoken to before."

"People! People! Attention ... attention please. Our agenda ..." Marcy waved her clipboard, raising her voice above the conversation.

"When he left the tennis ball ..." Mrs. Patel

started.

"Half of a tennis ball," her husband corrected.

"Yes, half of a tennis ball, Ravi and I remembered how long it's been since we've played tennis and how much we loved it. We dusted off our rackets, and it's been great getting back into it."

"According to Robert's Rules of Order, there should only be one person ..." Marcy was shouting now, but the chatter about the dog's antics continued.

"He left me a Kristin Hannah paperback," Mrs. Wilson said. "He trotted right onto my porch one afternoon, took a nice long doggie shake from nose to tail, and gently placed it on my welcome mat like a proud delivery dog. The book had a slip of paper in it that said 'Donate,' but I looked inside and saw it belonged to Liz Carter. I had to look up her address, but she's just down the street, and when I returned the book, I told Liz how much I love that author. We're starting a little book club if there are other fans who'd like to join."

Marcy dropped her notebook on the table and covered her head with her hands. She'd lost all control.

"We should have a neighborhood cookout," someone suggested from the back. "Keep tracking the dog, but make it a social thing. A dog watch party!"

Marcy shook her head in dismay as chatter broke out across the room. Her carefully prepared presentation about neighborhood security was being derailed by potluck planning. She stood by her PowerPoint, staring down at her discarded notebook as the conversation continued.

"What just happened?" she whispered when Harold approached.

Harold patted Marcy's shoulder. "I think you and that dog accidentally started something rather wonderful, Marcy."

She felt her face flush hot. This wasn't the reaction she'd anticipated after her meticulously prepared presentation. Her notes, her charts, her evidence—all ignored in favor of a book club and potato salad recipes. A strange emptiness swelled in her chest, a feeling that had become all too familiar over the years.

When Ben was around, they had friends, connections, but when he passed, she had withdrawn. She had alienated the people they were close to and now, enforcing the HOA rules was the only interaction she had with her neighbors. Without it, without her clipboard and her community log, who would she ever speak to?

She allowed herself to acknowledge what she had refused to accept: her notebook wasn't just about maintaining property values. It was the one thing that made people acknowledge her existence. The realization sent an uncomfortable pang through her chest. Fourteen years of meeting minutes carefully preserved, yet not a single invitation to a neighborhood barbecue tucked among them.

The community center door slid open. The familiar sandy-gold blur raced into the room, something brass and shiny clutched in its mouth.

"Well, I'll be," Harold chuckled. "The guest of honor himself."

The dog pranced proudly around the table, tail wagging like a metronome on fast-forward, a child's toy trumpet gleaming between his teeth.

"He's carrying a trumpet," Claire observed. "Clearly he's summoning us to battle."

"Or signaling his handlers!" Mr. Rodriguez suggested.

"Now, I probably shouldn't tell you this," Harold began, "but in my day, a trumpet like that could only mean one thing—"

"Murphy! Get back here you troublemaker!"

A young couple appeared in the doorway, slightly out of breath. The woman held a leash while the man carried a cardboard box labeled "DONATIONS."

"I'm so sorry," the woman said. "I'm Lila Harper, and this is my husband Eric. We moved in last month on Maple Street. Murphy got away while we were loading up some things to donate."

Eric lifted the box. "He keeps taking things out as fast as we put them in. The trumpet was supposed to go to the kids' music program."

Marcy's mouth fell open. Her precious notebook lay forgotten on the table, the pages fluttering in the breeze from the open door.

"You mean ... he's just a regular dog?" she

finally managed.

"Well, I wouldn't say regular." Eric laughed. "He's got a thing for collecting. The shelter told us he was found after a hurricane, carrying random objects from destroyed homes. They think he was trying to save things."

Murphy trotted over to Marcy and gently placed the toy trumpet at her feet, looking up at her with expectant eyes.

A realization washed over her. The rigid lines of her world softened, her shoulders drooped.

"He's ... bringing things to people," she said. "Not stealing."

"Yes," Lila nodded. "He's been making his rounds, hasn't he?"

Harold's voice broke through Marcy's thoughts. "You know, I think our friend Murphy here has been doing exactly what you've been trying to do all along, Marcy. Just with a different approach."

Marcy's eyebrows furrowed. "What do you mean?"

"Well, you both want a connected neighborhood, don't you? You with your rulebooks and meetings, him with his ... unconventional postal service."

Marcy looked at Murphy, who sat patiently at her feet. Was that what she wanted? A connected neighborhood? As she looked around the room at the animated faces, at people eagerly chatting with neighbors they'd barely acknowledged before, something within her shifted.

"I suppose we do want the same thing," she admitted.

"What if we had, like, regular neighborhood hangouts? And Murphy could be our mascot!" Jeremy said.

"Annual potlucks," Mrs. Rodriguez offered. "My patio is always open."

"And dog playdates," Lila added. "Murphy would love the company."

Marcy felt the familiar tightness returning to her jaw. The neighborhood's sudden enthusiasm for potlucks and playdates was threatening the orderly world she'd built, rulebook by rulebook.

Yet part of her—a part she rarely acknowledged —envied their easy camaraderie, their genuine connections.

"Now, Marcy," Harold said, patting her shoulder.

Marcy muttered, "He created chaos."

"Not chaos," Harold corrected. "Communication. Those relocated items did what twenty HOA newsletters couldn't. They got people curious, engaged, connected."

Harold leaned forward and continued. "What this neighborhood needs isn't just fun gatherings —though Lord knows we need those too. We need someone with organizational skills to coordinate it all. Someone who knows every bylaw and can help us navigate permits for block parties. "

Marcy's eyes widened slightly. "You mean ..."

"We need you, Marcy. But as a community

builder, not just a rule enforcer. That notebook of yours could track neighborhood participation instead of infractions."

The words settled over her like a warm blanket. For years, she'd used rules to force her way into the community, to make herself necessary. But what if there was another way to belong? A way that didn't require constant vigilance and enforcement?

"I suppose I could create a spreadsheet for tracking neighborhood engagement metrics," she said, but allowed a small smile to form. "Section 9 of the bylaws does authorize community-building initiatives."

Eric Harper, who had been quietly watching, spoke up. "You know, it's funny. We imagined he needed our help, yet Murphy's the one who seems to have brought the whole neighborhood together."

Murphy, as if understanding, looked around the room with those knowing eyes. When his gaze met Marcy's, she didn't see the chaos-causing canine menace she'd documented, but a creature who, like her, was simply trying to connect and protect the pieces of a community. Maybe Maple Creek Estates shouldn't be a testament to suburban uniformity, but a tapestry of suburban community. For some reason, that thought brought Ben to mind.

Marcy reached down and gently patted Murphy's head. "Well, I believe this meeting has been productive ... for once. And for the record, mister," she fixed Murphy with a stern gaze. "I'm pretty sure your tail wag alone violates at least two guidelines, but I'll let it slide—for now."

Three Minutes To Sunset

Marcus scrolled through the contest details *from StellarLens again, confirming that the $25k would be paid two weeks from the contest's conclusion. He checked the due date on the mortgage foreclosure statement.*

It'll all work out. We may need a little grace period from the bank, but it's going to be fine, he thought. *If it doesn't, it will take years for Sarah to forgive me ... if she ever does.*

The doorbell chimed. He dropped the bill and bolted to answer it, nearly tripping over Harper's scattered wooden blocks. He'd been tracking the package for days, refreshing the delivery status every few hours.

"Thank God," he whispered, signing for the package with a quick scribble.

Marcus cleared space on the coffee table by pushing aside the unpaid bills and Sarah's nursing textbooks.

He peeled back the packaging tape with meticulous precision. Inside, nestled in molded foam, was the StellarLens XF200—a marvel of engineering and optics. Marcus lifted the lens from its cradle, handling it like a newborn.

He carefully removed the lens cover. The glass elements gleamed with promise, untouched by fingerprints or dust. Replacing the cover, he tried the focus ring. It rotated with buttery smoothness beneath his fingers.

With this, he would finally capture the impossible shots that today existed only in his imagination. The StellarLens competition deadline was a week away, giving him plenty of time to dial things in and submit a winning shot–a green flash.

A bank statement peeked from beneath the scattered packaging, its bold red numbers momentarily catching his eye. The lens had cost nearly six months' worth of utility bills. Sarah had been furious when he'd explained the purchase.

Marcus pushed the thought away. Once he won, Sarah would understand. This wasn't an expense —it was an investment in their future.

Leaving the user's guide on the table, he carefully replaced the lens in its packaging. This would change their future; it would elevate his contest entry. They were after innovative composition, technical excellence, and emotional impact. With this glass, it was finally possible.

Sarah appeared from the hallway, balancing a

laundry basket against her hip, Harper's tiny socks and onesies peeking over the edge. Her eyes landed on the open shipping box resting atop the bills.

"It came," she said, her voice flat. Not a question.

"Yeah." Marcus shifted his weight from foot to foot. "It's even better than the reviews said."

"You know that just from unpacking it?" Sarah set the basket down beside the armchair with a soft thud and began folding clothing. "Two thousand dollars, Marcus."

"Only $1,949, actually. But the prize is twenty-five thousand."

"And if you don't win?" She folded a small yellow shirt with precise movements. "The mortgage has to be paid in like, two weeks, and we're already behind on the electric bill."

Marcus's jaw tightened. "This is my shot, Sarah. StellarLens launches careers. Last year's winner ..."

"I know. *National Geographic*." She tucked a strand of hair behind her ear. "I want that for you some day. I do. But right now, we need to keep the roof over our heads and the lights on."

"It's not just about the contest." The defensiveness in his voice surprised even him. "This is our future. Our way out of paycheck-to-paycheck."

Sarah's eyes softened. She placed her hand on his arm, the pressure gentle but firm. Marcus imagined it was meant to comfort him, but all he felt was her worry.

"I believe in your talent. Still, Harper needs stability more than her daddy needs a fancy lens."

The raw truth of her words stung.

A plaintive babble filtered through the baby monitor, followed by a delighted squeal. Marcus half-registered the sound.

Sarah disappeared down the hallway, her footsteps fading as she reached Harper's room. The monitor transmitted her gentle voice. "There's my big girl! Did you have a good nap?"

This lens would help him provide the stability that Harper, and Sarah, needed. He just knew it. He retrieved the user guide and began thumbing through the detailed exposure compensation ranges and diagrams of the internal element arrangement.

"Look who's up." Sarah appeared in the doorway with Harper whose hair stuck up in wispy tufts, her cheeks flush from sleep. "She pulled herself up in the crib and she's wanted to climb on everything all morning."

"Hmm? That's great." Marcus nodded without looking up. His finger traced the diagram showing the lens's focal plane. "Says here the minimum focusing distance is only eighteen inches. That's insane for a telephoto."

"She might walk any day now." Her voice had gone quiet.

"Yeah, she's growing up fast." The words left his mouth automatically, his attention still fixed on the manual.

"I thought you'd want to say 'Hi' after her nap. And I'm sure she would love to go back to the park tonight. Yesterday was so fun!"

"Hi, Harper." He glanced up briefly. Sarah bounced Harper gently, the baby reaching toward Marcus with pudgy fingers. "Can't go back to the park tonight, Daddy has some important work to do."

Marcus removed the XF200 from the box again. He grabbed his camera body from the shelf, removed the protective cap, and mounted the lens feeling that satisfying click as it locked into place. The combination looked professional. Serious. Award-winning.

His mind drifted to the quarry overlook he'd been researching for weeks. The perfect spot to capture the green flash at sunset. He'd need precise timing, perfect weather conditions, and now—he had the perfect lens. He imagined the shot: the sun setting, that rare emerald burst of light dancing above the horizon for just a few seconds. The judges would be stunned by his technical mastery, his patience, his vision.

Marcus Westgate, StellarLens Winner. The name would look good in print. *National Geographic* would call with a contract. His Instagram followers would multiply overnight.

"Marcus?" Sarah's voice broke through his reverie. "It would be good if you gave your daughter, and me, a bit of that attention. Also, remember you said you'd pick up my prescription before the pharmacy closes? They close at six today."

He pulled his gaze away from the viewfinder to glance at his watch without really seeing it. "Yeah, sure. I'll handle it."

"And you promised to grab something for dinner," she reminded him.

"I said I'll handle it," he repeated. He peered through the viewfinder, adjusting the focus ring; testing its smooth precision. "Just give me a minute to finish checking this out."

It was five days until the contest deadline. The weather hadn't cooperated at all, but Marcus wanted to take some test shots at the quarry. He guided his aging Honda up the winding road, leaning forward as the trees opened to reveal Limestone Quarry Overlook Park. Late afternoon sun slanted across the rolling farmland below, transforming ordinary fields into a patchwork of gold and amber. A weathered wooden sign marked the turnoff: "Historic Millford Quarry — Est. 1887."

The gravel parking area was dotted by a handful of cars. Several families were spread across the park, some with blankets on the grass others at the picnic tables. The children's play area was buzzing.

Marcus popped the trunk and assembled his

gear with practiced efficiency. He trekked away from the play area and picnic tables. He wanted perfect framing between the sloped quarry walls and also space to work undisturbed by curious onlookers asking questions about his equipment. He carefully mounted the camera and lens on his carbon fiber tripod, adjusting the legs to compensate for the slight incline of the quarry's edge.

The view stretched for miles. White limestone walls rising on either side of the vista caught the light, creating natural reflectors that would amplify the sunset colors. Marcus paced the area, calculating angles, mentally mapping the sun's trajectory. This spot offered an unobstructed western horizon—crucial for capturing the green flash at sunset.

He didn't want to leave anything to chance. He needed practice shots with a variety of settings and filters to make sure he had the lens down— placement, timing, filter choice. It all had to be perfect.

His phone vibrated in his pocket. Sarah, probably. Without looking, he silenced it.

He snapped several practice shots at a variety of settings. The StellarLens judges would see countless sunset shots. The green flash with this lens would set his entry apart, and he would only have a second or so to capture the life changing shot.

His stomach knotted as he considered the

variables beyond his control. One patch of haze, one bank of clouds on the horizon, one equipment failure—any of those, or countless other events, could ruin everything. Twenty-five thousand dollars and career-changing exposure hung on capturing two seconds of light.

His phone vibrated again—what was this, the fourth time in twenty minutes? He silenced the ringer again.

An uneasy knot formed in his stomach. Sarah knew he was working, and probably wouldn't call like that if it wasn't important, but this shot was important too. Still, what if something was really wrong with her or with Harper? He grimaced, keeping his eye pressed to the viewfinder. It could wait just a few more minutes.

The missed call notification sounded, then the phone began buzzing again nearly immediately. He snatched it from his pocket. His thumb hovered over the accept button, his stomach twisting with a pang of guilt. Five missed calls ... it couldn't be good.

"Sarah?" His voice cracked slightly. "I'm sorry. Everything all right? I know I've been ..."

He cut himself off, bracing for her response.

"Finally." Sarah's voice carried that tight, controlled quality that meant she'd been holding things together too long. "I've been calling for almost an hour."

"Sorry, I was just getting the test shots lined up, conditions aren't right tonight, but when they are,

I have to be ready. Everything okay?"

"Harper's on her last bottle and I've got a video meeting with my boss in fifteen minutes. We're out of formula and diapers. Can you please grab some and be home soon? I could really use a hand here."

Marcus checked the sun's position. The light was shifting to that golden hour glow, perfect for calibrating his settings.

"I just need a few more minutes to get these last test shots."

"Marcus." Her voice flattened. A clattering noise in the background, followed by Harper's fussing. "I've been solo parenting all day while prepping for this meeting. I need your help."

"Five minutes, that's all. This is important."

"And diapers and formula for your daughter aren't important?" Her words were sharp. He could picture the tension in her body. "You've been saying 'five more minutes' for days now. I need you here, and I need your help. I can't keep going like this … we can't keep going like this."

He framed another shot, watching light catch the limestone walls. So close to getting it just right.

"I'll leave in five, I promise. The CVS is on my way home."

"I need you to hear me. I will not keep going like this. If something doesn't change, I'll change it. I'll take Harper and we'll … we'll go somewhere … maybe to my parent's house."

"Hey, wait, I'm sorry." Marcus took a deep

breath, turning his back on the quarry overlook. "I know it's been crazy, but a couple more days and it will be over. We'll have the shot, and the prize money, and everything will be better."

"I don't want the shot. I want you." The anger had drained from Sarah's voice, her words barely a whisper now. She disconnected the call.

Marcus took a couple more deep breaths. When we have the money, things will be better. Once I get this contest behind me, and on my resume, things will change.

He turned his attention back to the last couple of test shots.

As the sun kissed the edge of the quarry wall casting long shadows across the limestone, he tilted the camera slightly. Through his viewfinder, the world transformed—ordinary fields became extraordinary, bathed in amber light that would never exist in quite the same way again. He pressed the shutter button, capturing the moment with a satisfying click.

"Perfect," he whispered, reviewing the images on the camera's display. The composition, the exposure, the clarity of the new lens—it all came together beautifully. He took three more shots with slightly different settings, insurance against any technical oversights.

Only when he finally stepped back from the camera did Marcus notice the time. Forty minutes had vanished. He scrambled to pack his equipment, suddenly aware of the emptying parking lot and lengthening shadows.

He dreaded checking his phone, and sure enough, three missed calls and a text from Sarah: "What happened to five minutes? My call was a disaster, and Harper's been fussy all evening. I'm ready to lose it!!!"

Guilt pinched his chest.

"Damn it," he muttered, stuffing the camera and expensive lens into his equipment bag.

Marcus sat at the kitchen table and diligently ignored the stack of bills that Sarah had arranged by priority, starting with the mortgage statement stamped "FINAL NOTICE" in red. The weather prediction had changed again, the forecasters now calling for a thirty percent chance of high clouds at sunset. His stomach tightened. High clouds would diffuse the light, potentially ruining any chance of capturing the green flash.

They always get it wrong, he thought. *They have to ... I just can't miss this shot. Too much is riding on it.*

The microwave beeped. Sarah placed a bowl of reheated pasta beside him, the ceramic clinking against the table's surface.

"Thanks," Marcus mumbled without looking up, intent on sunset time predictions now.

"Harper pulled herself up on the coffee table this morning," Sarah said, settling into the chair across from him. "You should have seen her face ... so determined. Just like her dad. And she's so confident standing there. I'm sure it won't be long before she lets go and takes off!"

"Mm-hmm," Marcus replied automatically. He glanced out the window at the sky. Which way were they predicting the cloud cover from again, south, or west? And it certainly looked crystal clear right now ... would that hang on?

"Remember our first apartment?" Sarah tried again, cutting Harper's lunch into tiny pieces. "How we used to watch the sunset from that terrible fire escape? You didn't even own a real camera then."

"Yeah ..." Marcus replied. He'd need to arrive at the quarry by 4:30 to set up properly.

Harper squealed from her play mat, babbling a string of almost-words. Marcus glanced up briefly as Harper rocked forward onto her hands and knees, wobbling as if she might push herself up.

Sarah leaned forward in anticipation. "She's trying to—"

"The clouds are moving in faster than predicted," he interrupted, showing her his screen. "I should head out early."

"You might as well, because you're not here again. I didn't head to my parents, but don't think I wasn't considering it ... seriously considering it. I can't live like this, and it doesn't seem to matter to you at all." Her voice was quiet but tense.

"It matters. When I win, we get twenty-five

thousand dollars." He pushed back from the table, defensive heat rising in his neck. "That solves everything. One perfect shot. This will finally put me on the map as a real photographer. I've been working toward this for years."

Sarah's laugh held no humor. "While our actual life is happening right here without you."

Harper cooed and murmured from her mat, oblivious to the tension crackling between them.

"You think I don't know that?" Marcus gestured at the bills. "You think I want to be struggling like this? The contest is our way out."

"No," Sarah said, her voice breaking slightly. "It's your hope for a way out."

Marcus rubbed his temples, the tension with Sarah making his head throb. He glanced at Harper, who was rocking on her play mat, tiny hands slapping the colorful fabric.

"Look, I know you're worried," he said, rising from his chair. "Let me just ..."

He crossed to Harper and scooped her up, partly to ease the tension, partly to escape Sarah's piercing stare. Harper's weight felt solid in his arms, her body vibrating with energy.

"Hey there, little miss photographer's assistant," he murmured, bouncing her gently.

Harper squealed, her legs pumping against his stomach. When he lowered her back to the floor she pulled herself upright holding his fingers with surprising strength. She teetered on rubbery legs, beaming with triumph, her eyes wide with the thrill of standing.

"Sarah, look … she's …"

His phone pinged loudly. The notifications showed an email from StellarLens: "FINAL DETAILS: Submissions close in 36 hours."

"Just a sec, Harper," he said, lowering her quickly back to the play mat. Harper scrunched her eyes and balled her tiny fists, starting to fuss.

"It'll be just a minute," he told himself, scanning the contest email.

Marcus caught Sarah's gaze across the room. Her eyes held that mixture of disappointment and resignation he'd seen more and more in the past few days.

Sarah held Harper by the waist as she squatted and pushed with her legs, trying out the muscles she'd been developing, her smile and babble returning. "You can't keep missing these moments," she said. "They don't come back."

Marcus moved to the hallway closet, pulling out his camera bag. "This contest isn't just another competition. Winners get noticed. They get opportunities."

He checked his watch—3:15. Perfect timing to arrive early and get set up and in position at the quarry. The afternoon light would give him time to test his settings before the golden hour approached.

"I'll be back after sunset with the picture that will change our future," he said, slinging the bag over his shoulder; it felt heavier than usual.

"Maybe we can watch a movie tonight?"

Sarah didn't answer. She just turned away, murmuring something to Harper about their afternoon plans.

Marcus hesitated at the door, the silence heavy between them. He wanted to say more—to make her understand that every hour at the quarry was an investment in their future. Instead, he just called out, "Love you both," and stepped outside.

Marcus arrived at the Limestone Quarry Overlook three hours before sunset. The prime western vantage point remained unclaimed— exactly as he'd hoped. He set his equipment on a weathered bench and breathed in the late afternoon air. The scent of honeysuckle floated on a light breeze.

"Perfect." He surveyed the horizon where the sun was making its descent. The atmospheric conditions looked promising—clear skies with just enough high-altitude moisture to create the refraction necessary for the green flash phenomenon.

As he mounted his camera on the tripod, adjusting the height with practiced precision, a family spread a blanket on the grass nearby. Their toddler squealed, chasing a butterfly while the parents laughed. Further back towards the picnic tables, teenagers tossed a frisbee, oblivious to the celestial event that would occur in just a few hours.

Marcus worked through the settings he'd decided on, installed the filter, and focused for a few test shots. His fingers moved with reverent confidence across the expensive new lens. This was what separated him from the others at the overlook—they came for recreation, a getaway; he came with purpose. They saw a park; he saw a canvas. They lived in moments; he captured them.

He was in his element, alone with his equipment and ambition.

Through the rest of the afternoon and into the evening, he continued to review his mental checklist. He had it down cold, nothing would interfere with the shot. The park crowd waxed and waned.

After he satisfied himself that he'd done all he could, that it was just a waiting game, he sat on the bench letting the late-afternoon sun warm his face. He imagined the perfect photo glowing on a magazine cover, promising an answer to his problems. But as the hours inched closer to sunset, the same light that would deliver his dream also reminded him of how quickly moments passed— moments he'd missed with Harper, phone calls he hadn't answered, nights Sarah had spent alone.

Maybe he had been disconnected, distanced, but this shoot had to be flawless. The golden hour approached, that magical time when sunlight turned honey-thick and photographers reaped their harvest.

His phone buzzed. It was Sarah. He felt guilty about how he had left things, but also didn't want to get into another big argument as the critical moment approached. He silenced the call and slid the phone back into his pocket.

A small voice nagged at the back of his mind, reminding him of the disappointment on her face that morning. Of Harper's tiny hands reaching for him from the play mat. Of the mortgage statement with its bold red lettering.

"Marcus!"

He froze, recognizing Sarah's voice instantly. Turning around, he saw her trudging up the path holding Harper with one hand and a backpack in the other. Her face was flush, her hair escaping its ponytail.

"What are you—" He checked himself, then restarted softer. "What are you two doing here?"

"I know how much this shot means to you," she said, easing the backpack from her shoulder with a sigh. "But I hated the way we left things—like we're on opposite sides. So I grabbed Harper, and we came to show you we're still in this together. Even if this moment isn't as important to me as it is to you, I want to be here when you capture it. We do, right Harper?"

Marcus glanced nervously between his camera and his family. "Um ..."

"We won't get in your way." Sarah set Harper down, pulled a blanket from the diaper bag, and spread it on the grass. "We just wanted to be with you."

Harper started crawling towards Marcus and the tripod.

"The light's changing every second," Marcus said. "I need to concentrate."

"Can I see?" Sarah asked, stepping closer.

"Not now." The words came out more forcefully than he intended. He softened his tone. "I have all the settings perfect, and I don't want to take any chances."

Sarah's smile faltered. She scooped up Harper and retreated to the blanket. Marcus pretended not to notice her hurt expression, his eyes fixed on the horizon, his mind counting minutes while the gap between them stretched wider than the quarry below.

He checked his watch. "Three minutes. We're in the home stretch." He'd practiced this countdown a hundred times. The air felt electric with possibility.

He hunched over the viewfinder, his world narrowed to the thin strip of horizon where sky met earth. The sun descended with agonizing slowness, its bottom edge kissing the horizon line.

From behind him, Harper squealed with delight. He could hear Sarah and her settling on the blanket. She seemed to have so much personality lately; her baby talk laced with attitude.

"Two minutes." His finger hovered over the

shutter release, heart hammering against his ribs. Everything—the mortgage, Sarah's worry, the contest deadline—condensed into this moment. He clicked off several shots, just to relieve some tensions.

He would finally feel like he was being the contributor he wanted to be; like he was being the husband and father, the provider, he wanted to be. One day, Sarah would appreciate it. So would Harper, even if all she wanted now was to play, and giggle, and bounce around on the grass.

"You are such a big girl." Sarah's quiet affirmation floated on the honeysuckle sweetened breeze.

"One minute."

He adjusted the focus ring with microscopic precision. The expensive glass of his new lens caught the golden light, transforming it into something magical in his viewfinder.

Just a bit longer and he wouldn't feel so pulled. Sarah was the practical one; he was the dreamer. She was the one that kept everything together, while he was scattered. She took everything to heart, while he was, maybe, too quick to jump ahead not paying as much attention to what he should.

He had to concentrate to hear Sarah's hushed words over the noise of the park. "Oh, there you go. You can do it."

"Thirty seconds," he whispered to himself. The conditions were perfect—clear sky, sharp horizon, stable air. If the green flash would appear anywhere tonight, it would be here, and then be captured forever.

He would have the shot, and hopefully the money, but was it really an investment, or was it a trade off? Sarah was the practical one. Was he fooling himself and risking the most important people in his life? Time never ran backwards, he would only get one shot at what came next, at how he chose to spend the next few seconds.

Get the shot, we're right here. Any second now.

He peered through the viewfinder, but strained to hear what Sarah and Harper were doing. A radio playing country music, cheers from the frisbee players, and the playground noise all washing across Sarah's encouragement.

"You're standing up," Sarah gasped. "All by yourself! You're huge, hot stuff."

Marcus's stomach dropped. His fingers froze on the camera. From the corner of his eye, he caught movement on the blanket where Sarah sat. Harper was standing, unaided, tottering on uncertain legs, her chubby arms extended toward Sarah.

Seeing his glance, Harper called, "Da." Her face was bright with determination.

Sarah, unaware that he was watching, whispered to Harper, "You're going to walk. You're going to take your steps!"

The sun slipped lower. Marcus spun back to the viewfinder. The conditions remained perfect for the green flash. His finger tensed on the shutter button.

But his daughter was about to walk for the first time.

He glanced at Harper again, then back through his viewfinder, the perfect shot framed exactly as he'd practiced. She was still smiling, oozing attitude, accomplishment mixed with fear.

The sun hovered at the critical position, seconds away from the green flash.

Marcus felt time splinter. On one path, he clung to the camera, chasing the dream that had nearly bankrupted his family. On the other, he let that dream go—just for a beat—and seized the moment his daughter was offering. His stomach twisted at the thought of losing either.

"Da!" Harper called again, her voice wavering with the effort of standing.

That tiny voice exploded his heart, broke through any doubt, and he realized he could rebuild finances, chase photos any time—but he'd never get these first steps back.

He turned from the camera as the sun slipped further into his perfect frame. The expensive lens, his ticket to recognition and success, temporarily forgotten.

"I'm here, sweetheart," he said, dropping to one knee next to Sarah and extending his arms. "You can do it. Look at you!"

Harper swayed, her tiny legs uncertain beneath her. She gained resolve, and took one trembling step forward, then another. Her face glowed with concentration and joy, each step more confident than the last.

Sarah gasped, covering her mouth with her hand.

Marcus smiled encouragement to his daughter. Harper tottered the final distance and collapsed into his waiting arms, giggling with triumph. He scooped her up and stood, spinning her around as she squealed with delight.

"You did it!" he cried, pressing his face into her soft hair.

"Marcus," Sarah whispered, pointing toward the horizon. "Look."

A flash of emerald light glimmered above the setting sun—the green flash, lasting barely a second before vanishing.

"You missed your shot," Sarah said, her voice thick with emotion.

A sharp ache twisted in Marcus's chest. That brilliant emerald flash he'd researched for months was gone. No more chances before the contest closed. He swallowed hard, pressing Harper closer, feeling her frantic little heartbeat against his ribs.

"Yeah," he whispered, kissing the top of her head, "I guess I did." Regret tugged at him for a fleeting moment, but the soft warmth in his arms reminded him this was the moment that really mattered.

He looked at Sarah, a weary smile curving his lips. "But I didn't miss what's most important."

Warm relief settled over him, lightening the

burden he'd carried for weeks. He knew, right then, that he'd choose this feeling—his family, their future—over any perfect shot.

The sun had vanished completely now, taking with it the green flash he'd chased for months. Golden light faded from the quarry, painting everything in soft purple shadows. Marcus cradled Harper against his chest, her small body warm and solid in his arms. He snuggled her giraffe blanket more tightly around her.

They'd taken turns, encouraging Harper to walk back and forth across the blanket between them until she had exhausted herself. It didn't take long, but her face had beamed with pride on each step.

Sarah moved beside him, her hand gentle on his shoulder. When he turned, her eyes shimmered with unshed tears and something else—relief, perhaps. The tension that had lived between them for weeks seemed to dissolve, for her at least, in the gathering twilight.

"Thank you for tonight. I'm sorry that you missed the shot, but I can't tell you when I last felt this close to you … when you last felt this close to us," she said, resting her head against their sleeping daughter and giving a hug that encircled them both.

If only this moment could last forever. But it

couldn't. It was the right choice, he knew it was, but the prize money was the solution he was banking on, and it was gone now. This feeling was amazing ... satisfying ... but the bills were still waiting at home.

What now? How would he ever ...

Sarah squeezed, as if sensing his anxiety.

"Don't go away again ... just be here," she whispered.

His daughter's first steps, the weight of her in his arms, and his wife holding him here as the evening darkened—this would never come again. Marcus breathed deeply, filling his lungs with evening air, the scent of fabric softener from the baby blanket, and the smell of Sarah's vanilla shampoo. He reeled himself back in from racing toward the next deadline ... the next milestone ... the next shot.

"I'm sorry for it all ... I lost sight of the things that should be most important to me," he said.

"You're here now ... and that's what matters."

Sarah stepped away and repacked the backpack then took Harper so that Marcus could gather his gear. They descended the limestone path away from the overlook together as the darkness thickened.

Marcus packed his gear into the trunk, pausing on the new lens for a minute, a grimace tightening his features. He tucked the backpack into the back seat of Sarah's car near the carseat. When he turned back from loading, he noticed Sarah, still holding Harper, was smiling.

"What?" he asked.

"Nothing. I've just missed you ... I've missed us," Sarah said, her voice lighter than it had been in weeks. "This ... to me, at least ... is worth so much more than winning a contest. This time together is worth so much more than the money."

"Yeah, well too bad this doesn't pay the bills. I just don't know how we're going to do it. I was so set on the contest. Stupid. Focused completely on the wrong thing."

For nearly a month the contest had consumed him, becoming the narrow tunnel through which he viewed his future. Standing here now, Marcus realized he had been focusing on the wrong subject all along. He'd been chasing perfection when what mattered most had been right beside him—messy, beautiful, and real.

He didn't know how they'd fix everything—not yet. But for the first time, he knew what not to lose.

"You know, I think I finally get it," he said, nodding slightly and pondering the realization.

"Get what?" Sarah leaned close, her face tilted toward him in the gathering darkness.

"Why we take pictures in the first place. It's not to own the moment. It's to remember we were part of it."

Harper sighed in her sleep. Above them, more stars emerged, bearing silent witness to this perfect, unphotographed moment.

Margin Notes

I'm supposed to clock out at eleven, but honestly, I've been checked out since about 2018. I scrub the counter, my rag making sad squeaking noises against the laminate. The clock above the register reads 10:57.

Living the dream—if the dream involves wiping up someone else's chai to complete my evening.

Anna bailed two hours ago. Whatever. The tip jar holds exactly eleven dollars and thirty-seven cents, which is a measly five-something once I factor out her share, and assuming I want to split the buck that came in after she left. Not even enough for a decent meal, let alone making any dent in this month's rent.

The espresso machine sits half-cleaned, gurgling occasionally like it's laughing at me. I should finish prepping it for tomorrow's opening crew, but honestly, what's the point? They'll just dirty it again in eight hours.

The wall clock clicks to 11:00. Freedom.

I toss the rag toward the sink but my aim sucks. I reach to grab the rag, and see the lost-and-found bin under the counter. Company policy says we keep stuff for thirty days before it gets donated. Most of it's junk—single gloves, scratched sunglasses, so many umbrellas, a plastic barrette with Hello Kitty missing an ear.

For some reason, though, I decide to scavenge.

As expected, it's full of worthless crap. Then I notice a paperback, dog-eared and coffee-stained. The cover shows some ethereal-looking tree against a sunset. Roots of Being: Finding Your Authentic Path. I snort. Sounds like something my last manager would've forced us to read in a team-building exercise.

I flip through it anyway, landing on a page where someone's scribbled in the margin. The handwriting slants right, blue ink pressed hard into the paper: "Let it stay messy." Yeah, someone gets it.

Then I notice they've underlined a passage in the text: "The soul seeks shape."

They must have realized how stupid that line is and tried to put things right. They didn't go far enough, the original line doesn't deserve to exist at all! I grab the Bic from the counter and finish the deed with a big, black X.

God, people write in books like they're talking to the universe. No wonder nobody wants this one back.

I start to toss it back in the bin but pause, the

book hovering above the pile of other orphaned junk.

Can't say why, but I glance out the shop's front windows, scanning the empty sidewalk. The late-night bus rumbles past, empty except for a single passenger lump slumped in the seat.

I slide the book into my bag with the granola bar I meant to eat for lunch.

The espresso machine gives one final gurgle. I turn off the lights and lock up.

Outside, the night air hits cold and damp. My breath fogs in front of me as I trudge three blocks over. The building looms ahead, cheap apartments above an abandoned laundromat. Home sweet home.

Two flights up I fumble with keys that never want to work on the first try.

I drop my bag onto the couch, unlace my boots, and kick them off. They land with satisfying thuds against the wall. The radiator clanks and hisses, fighting a losing battle against the draft from the windows.

Two steps over and I collapse on the bed, the convenience of a one-room apartment— everything you need all crammed no more than a pace away.

I stare at the cracked landscape on the ceiling, trying to decide if I'm going to explore the science experiment that is the fridge or skip dinner, close my eyes, and surrender until tomorrow.

While oblivion sounds appealing, I can't. I grab

my bag and dump everything out on the bed. Wallet. Keys. Phone. Chapstick. The granola bar, old but probably still safer than the fridge. And there it is—the stupid book.

Why did I even bring you home? You're just a crappy self-help book.

I pick it up and open to the same page again. The soul seeks shape.

The soul seeks shape ... What, like a Pinterest vision board? No thanks.

Let it stay messy.

Something about those two ideas—the printed text versus someone's handwritten rebellion— makes my skin itch.

Why am I letting some random book get to me? It's just words. Meaningless, mass-produced garbage.

I hurl it across the room. It hits the wall with a satisfying slap before falling down behind the TV stand.

Good. Let it stay there.

I grab the remote and click on the TV to anything, throw myself back on the bed, and grab my phone.

The third episode of something mindless plays while I swipe through photos of people I barely knew in high school. Someone got engaged. Someone had twins. Someone else bought a house with a yard that doesn't look like a crime scene.

I click the phone dark. Dump the TV. Close my eyes. Back to the phone. Try TV again. Nothing holds.

"This is pathetic."

The ceiling landscape hasn't changed—I'm still right here. Three hours wasted. I glance to the corner where the book landed, its spine barely visible behind the TV stand.

The soul seeks shape.

I grab my pillow and press it over my face, groaning into the fabric. "Shut up, shut up."

The book doesn't respond, obviously. But it's there radiating annoyance, like the whine of a mosquito, across my apartment.

Three hours of nothing, and I still can't kill the signal from one stupid line.

With a huff, I roll off the bed and cross the room. I fish the book from behind the TV stand and turn it over in my hands.

"Fine. You win."

The pages fall open exactly where I expect. Like the book remembers. Like it's been waiting.

The soul seeks shape.

Shape like what? Inspirational fridge magnets and a skincare routine?

I trace the handwriting in the margin like I'm writing it myself: Let it stay messy.

Someone cared enough about these words to argue with them. To make them personal.

I go to the front of the book. June Lin is written

in that same slanting, pretty, perfect, annoying handwriting on the inside of the front cover.

Why the hell did you underline that, June? My next bizarre thought is: I wonder if June looks like me?

"And what does 'messy' mean to you? What does that look like?"

The question hangs in my apartment. June's not here to answer.

I thumb through more pages, scanning for something else to hate. There are plenty of choices; blue ink scattered throughout, stars next to paragraphs, brackets around sentences, little exclamation points in margins.

"People find meaning in such worthless crap." I skim faster now.

Authentic connection requires vulnerability.

"Hard pass."

The greatest risk is never taking one.

"Fortune cookie garbage."

But the first line keeps circling back. The soul seeks shape. Let it stay messy.

I snap the book closed and press it against my forehead. "God, shut up already."

I wake with a gasp at 5:17 AM, my face feels flushed and the creases of my elbows and neck are sweat damp. The book lies open on my chest like a dead bird. I must have fallen asleep reading it. I push it off onto its own side of the bed and June's handwriting catches the weak light.

I'm irritated ... chased. I need light.

Kicking off the tangled sheets, I stumble past the framed Ochre Drift concert poster to the window and yank the blinds open. The sky hangs in that weird pre-dawn limbo—not night, not morning, just the weird, gray oatmeal color in between.

My apartment feels wrong. Too still. Like it's holding its breath, waiting for something.

"This is stupid." My voice sounds thin against the silence. What the hell is happening to me?

The walls press in, suddenly claustrophobic. I need out. Now.

I grab my jacket, almost reach for my headphones—then stop. For once, I don't want the buffer. I want ... what? To hear whatever's making me feel this way?

I walk with no direction, hands shoved in pockets, shoulders hunched. The cold air slaps my face. The streets are empty except for a delivery truck idling at the corner market. No playlist, no podcast—just the scrape of my boots on concrete and distant traffic hum.

It's weird. Unsettling. I always drown out the world.

A few blocks in, my breathing steadies. My thoughts slow down. The sky shifts from gray to pale blue, and suddenly light spills across a wall ahead—some artist's sprawling mural half-covered in tags. Morning hits the colors and they glow against the brick, orange bleeding into purple.

"Huh." The sound escapes before I can stop it.

Maybe I'm walking because I'm losing my mind. Maybe it's sleep deprivation. Maybe it's a quarter-life crisis right on schedule.

Or maybe the book's margin note is actually getting to me. Maybe I'm seeking some change—a slightly different shape.

Later, back at work, the afternoon shift crawls by in its usual caffeine-fueled haze. I've set my phone down, face-down. Just for a bit. Call it a detox, a personal challenge, or whatever.

"Medium drip, room for cream." I don't even look up as I complete the order for our only customer.

As they walk away, I have the urge to grab my phone. It's a habit. I resist. By the thirty-second mark though, I'm questioning all my life choices.

I give in and snatch up the phone. Three updates. None worth the twitch. Not so good on the detox, I guess, but I'm not a junkie, I can quit anytime I want.

But I'm already scrolling. Like the feed might forget me if I don't check in.

I slam the phone down again. Reset. Try harder.

Between customers, I distract myself. I stare

at the chalkboard menu until the words blur. The ceiling tiles. The scratched countertop. Anything.

Staring at nothing is harder than doomscrolling. Who knew?

"The soul seeks shape." Ugh. That line again. Every time it comes back, I feel like I need it, but it would be easier if I understood what it was. Not what the book says it is, but what it is to me, in my life.

Maybe it's about … structure? Some crap about how we need boundaries to be free? Or maybe it's about being willing to be seen—taking form instead of dissolving into digital noise.

"Let it stay messy," though. That part I get. That part I live. The contradiction feels right. Like maybe the point isn't having it all figured out—just not ghosting your own life.

I catch myself deep in thought and laugh. Since when do I philosophize during shifts?

I'm paroled early this evening, but now the stifling silence of my apartment feels like a crowded elevator or a funeral parlor—someone say something already. I jump at the vibration of my phone on the table. Jake's name shows up. A familiar feeling washes over me—not excitement, not even interest really. Just habit.

hey u up for tonight? my roommate's gone till sunday

My thumbs hover over the keyboard. Two days ago, I wouldn't have hesitated. Three drinks at his place, conscience dampened, the comforting numbness of it all. I'd leave before morning light, another night successfully killed.

I type: sure what time

Then delete it.

I type: can't tonight, maybe

Delete that too.

I click the screen black without responding and stare at my reflection in it. The silence of the apartment wraps around me, not suffocating anymore. Just ... there. Like it's waiting to see what I'll do with it.

I cave and unlock the phone. My usual answer would be so easy—say yes, go over, let my body run on autopilot while my mind checks out. Wake up hollow but safely numb.

I lock the phone again, with resolve.

Hours pass. My phone buzzes twice more. I don't check it. I heat up ramen. Read three pages of the book, put it down. Pick it up again. The margin notes keep pulling me back.

By midnight, I'm still alone in my apartment, laying on the bed looking up. No Jake. No hookup. No escape.

"I didn't go," I say to the empty room. "I didn't die. Noted."

The ceiling offers no response. The landscape hasn't changed. I'm still right here, but I wonder if there's something I've been running from all this time. A void I was filling with bodies and booze and endless scrolling?

Maybe there's something else. Some hunger that cheap distractions can't touch. Something that wants ... shape.

The thought makes me uncomfortable. Admitting you need something means admitting you give a crap. I never have.

Ready to give up consciousness for the night, I roll over and assume the usual position facing the window, when I notice it—the concert poster I hung two years ago when I first moved in is tilted, the right corner higher than the left. Has it always been that way? I've looked at it a thousand times without seeing it.

The lopsided angle suddenly irritates me. Like an eyelash caught under a contact lens.

Screw it. I turn over. That lasts for thirty seconds. Fine. I cross the room and stand in front of the poster, like from here it will suddenly be straight. It's not. I nudge the right side down slightly.

I step back. The poster—Ochre Drift, I haven't listened to their crap in years—looks different now. Intentional?

It's stupid. How can straightening a picture make the room ... righter? But it does.

The space feels ... I don't know. Better? The thought is embarrassing, but true. This crooked frame that I've ignored for years was whispering chaos all this time, and until tonight, that was fine with me ... but now, righter is better.

I run my palm over the frame once more, feeling a small, strange satisfaction. I've adjusted its shape. The parallel hits me, and I can't help but laugh. A small laugh, but not a cringe one.

I oversleep. My phone alarm blares three times before I smack it into silence. My head feels clearer than usual—no hangover, just the residual fog of actual sleep.

The counter reveals my last instant oatmeal packet lurking behind an ancient box with like five Cheerios. Too dangerous. Grocery run on the way to work it is.

Panda Market sits two blocks from my apartment, a fluorescent-lit rectangle with inconsistent stock and surprisingly good produce. I grab my usual: instant oatmeal, ramen, coffee, and three bananas—that seems to be the magic number for me.

At the register, a man in a faded work jacket counts coins with trembling fingers. The cashier waits, expressionless. The line behind us grows.

"Three twenty-seven," the cashier repeats, slower this time.

The man's weathered hands spill pennies across the counter. "I'm sorry, I thought I had—" His voice is barely audible.

I shift my weight, eyes fixed on the exit.

Normally I'd stare at my phone, pretend this human struggle isn't happening three feet away.

"I can come back later," he murmurs, sliding the grocery bag towards the clerk.

My hand moves before my brain catches up. I flash my phone at the reader and it beeps. Done. "There."

His eyes meet mine—startled, embarrassed, grateful.

"Don't make it a thing. It's not a thing," I shrug.

The guy clutches his grocery bag against his chest. "You didn't have to do that."

"Didn't want to stand here all day." The words come out sharper than intended.

He doesn't flinch or walk away. Instead, he studies my face with a steady gaze that makes my skin prickle. Not creepy-staring, but actually seeing. Like he's memorizing something important.

"Well, thank you." His voice carries a weight that three dollars and change doesn't deserve.

I shove my groceries onto the belt to move him along. "No big deal."

"It is to me," he says.

The sincerity in his voice catches me off guard. My throat tightens. This wasn't supposed to be a moment. Just a transaction. A blip in the day. Not ... whatever this is becoming.

"Yeah, well." I flash my phone again for my crap, load it in my backpack, and sling it over one shoulder. "Have a good one."

As I push through the door, a strange warmth creeps across me. I tell myself it's just the sun hitting my face—not the echo of someone saying thank you like it mattered.

It wasn't about the time. Or the line. I just did it. And now it's sitting with me, reshaping the silence I thought I'd made peace with.

The afternoon shift at Daily Drip stretches before me like a desert with no oasis. Worse, I'm stuck with Anna, who bounces in wearing a sunflower-patterned shirt that practically screams at customers to have a nice day.

"Ren! Did you see we got those new seasonal syrups?" She taps her fingers against the counter in rapid succession. "The pumpkin one smells exactly like fall should."

I line up the sugar packets without thinking, smoothing the edge of the napkin holder with my sleeve. "Fascinating," I mutter, though it comes out less sharp than usual.

"Are you organizing stuff now?" Anna tilts her head, studying me like I'm a science experiment. "This a new hobby or a cry for help?"

Kill me now. She's an emotional TED Talk with an apron.

"Just caffeinated." I retreat to restock the straw bins—unnecessary busy work to escape whatever heartfelt conversation she's brewing.

"Well, I think it's nice." She follows me, undeterred. "Sometimes tiny shifts mean we're growing."

I close my eyes briefly, summoning patience. Two more hours of this. Two more hours of Anna's relentless positivity radar picking up signals that aren't there.

"The only thing growing is my student loan interest," I mutter.

Anna laughs like I've said something profound instead of bitter. "That's why I love working with you. So real."

I busy myself with the straw bins, hoping Anna will take the hint and drift away. But instead of her usual bounce, she leans against the counter with a sigh that seems to deflate her entire body.

"My mom would've loved these seasonal things." Her voice drops to a register I've never heard from her. "She collected mugs from every coffee shop we visited. Said each one held memories."

The unexpected shift catches me off guard. I glance over my shoulder, unsure what to do with this version of Anna—the one without the exclamation points.

"She passed away three years ago. Cancer." Her fingers tap once, twice, then stop altogether. "Some days I still set a second mug."

The words hang between us, honest and raw. I could brush past it, make some comment about the afternoon rush. Instead, I find myself turning around.

"I used to do that for my brother. Different reason. Same ghost." The confession slips out before I can catch it. "He left when I was fifteen. Never really said goodbye."

Anna doesn't rush to fill the silence with platitudes or questions. She just nods, her eyes meeting mine without the usual sparkle of forced cheer.

"Ghosts are stubborn," she says finally.

"Yeah." I return to the straws, but slower now. "They are."

The quiet between us feels different—not awkward, just ... real. I can't remember the last time I had a conversation that wasn't wrapped in three layers of sarcasm. Or alcohol.

The hours blur like usual, but I don't feel like screaming into the mop closet, so that's new. Anna doesn't push for more confessions, and I don't offer any. But something's shifted—like furniture rearranged in a dark room. You can't see it, but you feel the difference when moving through the space —the shape is different.

I even find myself not minding when she hums along to the shop's playlist.

Walking home, I can't get Anna out of my head. The cheerful coworker with the floral wardrobe and collection of inspirational quotes. Easy to dismiss. Easier to mock. But underneath all that brightness was someone carrying the same kind of hollow space I recognize.

I'd assumed her positivity was ignorance—turns out it's a choice. Maybe even a hard-won right.

I thought she was fluff. Now I realized in her own way, she's stitched together like the rest of us.

The book's text and margin note float back: The soul seeks shape. Let it stay messy. I roll that around without immediate rejection. What shape have I been forcing myself into? The shape that jokes first, ghosts second, and never asks for anything real?

The shape that sees instant distraction from my phone and instant gratification from my 'friends?'

But my shape adjusted today—bent slightly toward someone else's pain instead of away from it. And it didn't kill me. Didn't even hurt.

I pause at the crosswalk, watching people stream past. They all look so put together, like being alive isn't a constant improv act. I used to call that delusion. Now I'm thinking maybe I've been deluding myself.

Inside the apartment I turn the lights on but leave the TV off. The silence feels deliberate rather than empty.

I grab the book from where I'd tossed it on the counter and stretch out on the bed.

The soul seeks shape.

"Let it stay messy," I whisper the margin note aloud.

These words shouldn't matter. Some random person's scribbles shouldn't be rearranging my mental furniture. Yet here I am, in my apartment without the usual noise buffer between me and my thoughts.

I grab a pen and turn to a blank page near the back. The pristine paper waits, patient and judgmental all at once.

My pen hovers. I write: This whole soul-searching thing is just boredom mixed with caffeine withdrawal. Tomorrow I'll be back to normal.

I read it over and recognize my dishonesty. Cross it out with three harsh lines that tear slightly into the paper.

I try again: Today I listened instead of tuning out.

I stare at the words, my handwriting isn't as nice as June's, but the confession sits there, undeniable.

Let's be clear—I haven't seen the light. I just ... stopped sprinting in the dark for a second.

I add: Anna carries her mother in coffee mugs. I carry my brother in silence. Different shapes, same hollow.

I'm not sure if I'm writing or admitting

something I've spent years avoiding. My hand trembles. This honesty thing is worse than a hangover. I press the pen harder against the page, like I'm trying to convince myself.

I don't know what I want. But I know it's not nothing.

The words stare back at me, simple and terrifying. I've never admitted that before, not even to myself.

I close the book.

All those nights scrolling through videos of people I'll never meet. The endless stream of content that evaporates the moment I swipe past. The hookups that blur together, faces I couldn't pick out of a lineup a week later.

What shape does any of that have?

Anna talks about her mother with such clarity —the smell of her perfume, how she stirred sugar into coffee. Meanwhile, I've been filling my life with static, calling it freedom.

I've been so busy mocking other people's substance that I never noticed my own hollowness. The irony cuts deep—I accused Anna of being superficial when I'm the one skimming the surface of everything.

My phone sits dark on the table. For once, I don't reach for it.

I retreat to the bed, lay the book across my chest, and stare up at the ceiling. As I drift off to sleep, the landscape of cracks looks different. It's shifted. Something seems new.

The alarm cuts through my dream, dragging me back to consciousness much too soon. I reach for my phone and dismiss the alarm with the practiced motion of someone who's spent years avoiding the morning.

The book lies beside me. I stuff it into my bag.

Early shift today.

I arrive at the coffee shop thirty minutes before opening. The silence feels almost sacred—no hissing espresso machine, no mumbled orders, just the faint hum of refrigerators and early morning light filtering through dusty windows.

I move to the lost and found box tucked beneath the counter. It's still filled with the same junk. In another two weeks it will all get donated.

Before placing the book inside, I open to the last page. I grab the Bic and scratch in one final thought: "Still messy. But I think messy is a shape in progress."

Someone once scribbled their thoughts unaware of how they might affect someone else. Now I'm doing the same—casting a message into the void without expectation.

I put the book into the box, tucking it between a navy scarf and a smiley face keychain with no keys. Someone might find it tomorrow. Or never. That part isn't up to me.

The morning rush floods in, and I fall into

the usual rhythm of orders and change. But something's off. Not in a bad way—just … off.

My phone stays in my pocket. Not because I'm making a point. Just because the quiet feels less like a void, and the buzzes feel less like proof I exist.

On break, I catch myself watching one of our regulars get his drink, take it to his seat, and just sit for a beat—eyes closed, hands wrapped around the cup like it's a ritual. I always thought people like that were faking it. Now I'm not so sure. Maybe he's just … aware of the moment in a way I never let myself be.

That stupid book really messed with my head. Thanks, June.

I'm still me. Still allergic to morning people. Still think "Live, Laugh, Love" should be a prosecutable offense. But maybe there's space to notice things; to do more than skim the surface of life from one distraction or high to the next. To let a little clarity in around the edges. Maybe not everything worth feeling has to come with a dopamine hit or a neon sign.

And maybe—just maybe—some of life isn't as dumb as I thought. Maybe shape doesn't have to mean surrender of who I am, or conformity, but instead is an honest expression–me really living out loud.

The Ark On Bramble Hollow Drive

*J*une 3rd. *Dear Diary, something weird is happening next door.*

Molly tucked herself deeper into her blanket fort, balancing her diary on her knees. Her pink flashlight cast a rosy glow across her deepest thoughts. Mr. Wiggles, her one-eyed teddy bear, watched from his sentry position by her pillow.

She listened to the steady thunk-thunk-thunk coming from across the fence. The sound had started three days ago and hadn't stopped, even when Mom said normal people should be sleeping.

Molly peeled the blankets back and peeked through her curtains. There he was again—Mr. Ames, hammering away under his porch light. The curved wood looked like—

It's a BOAT! she wrote, underlining it twice. *But*

there's no water here. Not even a swimming pool.

She chewed her pencil. "Maybe he's building a Noah Boat."

Mom's voice drifted up the stairs. "Yeah, Franklin next door has finally lost it, Jen. Building a boat in his backyard. A boat! We're three hundred miles from the ocean."

Molly frowned. Grown-ups always thought they knew everything. Molly didn't think Mr. Ames was crazy. He was nice. Maybe he just wanted to have a boat. She wished she could make something special like that.

She flipped to a fresh page in her diary and grabbed her colored pencils. A boat took shape on the paper—brown curved sides, just like Mr. Ames was building. She added blue swooshes for waves, then paused.

What if it wasn't for water at all?

She sketched feathery wings sprouting from both sides of the boat, colored them yellow and purple.

"Maybe it's for flying instead of swimming," she whispered to Mr. Wiggles.

* * *

June 5th. Dear Diary, I did something brave yesterday. I left Mr. Ames a note by his fence. Just a small one that said 'Is it for the flood?' because maybe he's like Noah and knows something important.

She paused, tapping the pen against her chin. The memory of sneaking to the fence while Mom was on the phone made her feel like a spy on a mission.

He didn't write back, but this morning when I checked, there was a tiny wooden star stuck on the fencepost! It wasn't there yesterday. It's so perfect and smooth, like a real star that fell from the sky.

Molly glanced at the little carved star she'd placed on her windowsill.

I think he knows I know. She underlined each word carefully. *About the boat being special.*

Her heart fluttered like the butterflies she'd seen in the garden. Someone else believed in magic too.

* * *

Today she wrote in deep blue colored pencil. *June 7th. Dear Diary, Last night I dreamed about the boat next door.*

She paused, chewing her bottom lip, searching for the right words.

We were floating in it—me, Mr. Wiggles, a giraffe, and two penguins. Mr. Ames stood at the front, not saying anything, just pointing at clouds that looked like faces.

Molly sketched a quick cloud with eyes in the margin.

The weird part was we didn't go anywhere. But we did. She underlined the sentence twice. *Like we were moving without moving.*

She tapped the pencil against her chin, remembering the feeling.

I think I figured it out! Her handwriting grew bigger with excitement. *The boat isn't supposed to MOVE places. It's for carrying FEELINGS. Like how sometimes my chest feels too full and I need somewhere to put everything.*

* * *

"Would you look at that." Harlen gestured with his beer bottle toward the neighboring yard. "Day sixteen of whatever the hell Ames is doing over there."

He settled deeper into his sagging deck chair, the aluminum frame creaking in protest. The late afternoon sun cast long shadows across his backyard, illuminating the top of Franklin's fence and—more irritatingly—the wooden skeleton rising behind it.

Milton leaned forward in his chair, adjusting his thick glasses. "Looks like a boat to me."

"In central Missouri." Harlen snorted. "Franklin's building a yacht in the most landlocked spot in America."

They watched as Franklin moved with methodical precision around the curved hull. No wasted motion. No hurry. Only the continuous motion of saw on wood then hammer on nail that had become the soundtrack to Harlen's afternoons.

"Maybe he knows something we don't." Milton's voice was flat, impossible to read.

"Yeah, like how to waste your retirement."

Harlen took a long pull from his beer, but the usual satisfaction didn't come. Something about Franklin's quiet dedication needled him. "Man hasn't said a word to anyone in weeks. Just ... building."

"Hmm," was all Milton said.

Harlen tapped his bottle against the armrest. "Bet you fifty bucks he abandons it before the month's out. Everyone starts projects. Nobody finishes them. And when he does, he better not leave it there. The last thing I want to do is look at that all summer!"

* * *

Darkness settled over Bramble Hollow Drive, but Harlen couldn't sleep. He found himself standing at his back fence, peeking over the weathered wood.

Franklin worked by lantern light. The man's movements carried the same unhurried precision they had that afternoon, but something about the night transformed the scene. The boat's ribs curved upward, skeletal but with promise; blooming, not decaying.

The lantern swung gently as Franklin moved from place to place, sending light dancing across the half-formed hull. Wood grain caught the glow, revealing amber depths and honey-colored whorls Harlen hadn't noticed before.

Harlen's throat tightened. He'd built things before—a bookshelf, a birdhouse, projects abandoned in his garage. But this ... this was different. Franklin worked like a man translating something from inside himself, each nail and joint speaking what his voice wouldn't.

The night air carried the scent of fresh-cut cedar. Harlen inhaled deeply, surprised by a sudden longing for a challenge.

He let go of the fence and took a step back, a half-forgotten memory surfacing. The newspaper clipping. Franklin Ames, twenty years younger but with the same steady eyes, standing outside a charred two-story house, oxygen mask dangling from his neck.

The headline flashed in Harlen's mind: LOCAL FIREFIGHTER RETURNS TO BLAZE FOR TRAPPED FAMILY.

Harlen remembered Franklin's quote—the only one in the article: "I heard them. That's all." Five words to explain running back into a collapsing building. The paper called him a hero.

It wasn't like they were close neighbors; they'd talked maybe a dozen times over the years. Once about property lines when Harlen first moved in. A few times about the weather. That day Franklin's wife died, when Harlen awkwardly offered to mow his lawn.

When the Rodriguez boy's bike was stolen, Franklin appeared with a replacement. No note, no explanation. He just propped the bike against their porch and left. His mother would never have known it was Franklin had Harlan not told her.

He rubbed the back of his neck. Franklin had always been like this—moving through the world with quiet certainty while the rest of them talked in circles.

What ever put this crazy boat idea in his head?

The sound of a hammer striking wood echoed through the darkness. Precise. Purposeful. Familiar.

The hammer's rhythm followed Harlen back to his house. Inside, the silence pressed against him. His living room looked exactly as it had for the past eight years—recliner angled toward the television, remote on the side table, yesterday's coffee mug still there.

He flicked on the light and caught his reflection in the darkened window.

"What the hell am I doing with my days?" The words slipped out, barely audible even to himself.

His weekly routine played through his mind: Monday poker, Wednesday coffee with Milton, Thursday beers, weekend TV. The same conversations, the same complaints, the same stories told and retold until they'd worn smooth as river stones.

The image of Franklin's hands working the timber returned, his hands moving with purpose, building something that might never float but existed because he willed it into being.

Harlen's chest tightened with … what? Envy? Not envy for the boat itself, but for the quiet purpose behind every swing of Franklin's hammer.

* * *

June's slippers scraped across the kitchen tile as she navigated through darkness broken only by the digital clock's blue glow: 3:17 AM. She dropped bread into the toaster and depressed the lever, sounding the starter's gun of her morning routine. The machine's mechanical click and hum filled the quiet house.

When the toast popped, she slathered it with butter, then carried her plate to the kitchen window. Standing there, she could see most of the neighborhood—dark houses with darker yards, the occasional porch light creating islands of visibility.

Except for the yard kitty corner to hers.

The old guy was out there with sandpaper, working the curved side of what was undeniably becoming a boat. Each stroke was methodical, unhurried. No frustration. No pause. Just the continuous motion of someone chasing a goal.

June took a bite of toast, chewing slowly as she watched.

"Still at it." There was no one in the house to hear, nobody to disturb.

Three nights later, June found herself at the same window, same toast, same view. The planking on the hull was higher, but bare ribs still arched upward like a whale's bones excavated from the soil.

A week passed. The hull grew smoother,

higher, more defined. She saw another change—new supports, the beginnings of a small cabin. Progress on the boat she noticed keenly, while her shifts at the hospital blurred together—same patients, different names. Same procedures. Same paperwork.

Two nights later. The cabin was well formed. When did that guy sleep? Didn't he ever stop? He was dedicated, that's for sure. Unrelenting.

"I used to write." She thought of her novel, *The Weight of Quiet Things*, still unfinished on her laptop. Lately, all she wrote were patient notes ... and grocery lists.

Outside, that old guy's hands never stopped moving.

* * *

Pastor Mike Reed came armed with warm banana bread.

This wasn't just a visit—it was what shepherds did. When one sheep strayed, you went. You showed up.

As he walked up the driveway toward Franklin's backyard, he murmured words from First Corinthians.

"If one member suffers, all suffer together ..."

The words dissolved as the backyard came into view. There sat Frank Ames, perched in the skeleton of his unfinished vessel. Not hammering. Not measuring. Not working at all. Just sitting, spine straight as a mast, facing forward toward some invisible horizon.

Mike stopped in his tracks. Frank looked like a sea captain awaiting a storm, though the boat remained landlocked, unfinished, improbable.

"Permission to come into the yard, Captain?" He called.

Frank didn't move ... didn't even look in his direction.

The gate creaked as Mike tentatively pushed it open, stepping onto Frank's property with careful reverence.

He cleared his throat gently. "Brought banana bread. Thought maybe you could use a little something sweet."

Frank didn't turn, but nodded slowly.

Mike hesitated, sensing he'd arrived in the middle of something quietly significant. Not just a project, but a kind of devotion.

Mike set the bread on a nearby sawhorse, noticing again the still-warm foil. The words he'd rehearsed felt suddenly out of place, like formal attire at a fishing dock.

"You know, some folks are starting to wonder ..." he offered, voice trailing into the evening air.

Frank lifted one hand and rested it on the side of the boat's frame pressing against the wood with a peculiar tenderness, as if he were drawing strength and encouragement from his creation.

Mike shifted his weight. His shirt collar felt tight despite being unbuttoned. He'd counseled through silences before—grief-stricken pauses, angry stillness, contemplative quiet. This was different. This silence wasn't uncomfortable because it was empty—it was uncomfortable because it seemed full.

He forced a soft chuckle. "Bit of a Noah thing?"

No reply. Just the rustle as Frank adjusted slightly in his seat, eyes fixed ahead at nothing Mike could see. The pastor's words hung in the air between them.

Mike studied the boat for the first time without judgment. The curve of the hull swept upward with unexpected grace. A small cabin adorned the deck. Not the rough-hewn monstrosity he'd pictured when describing the incident to his wife, but something ... beautiful. Crafted with care rather than obsession.

As he focused on the boat, a peculiar sensation washed over him. The backyard seemed to tilt beneath his feet, the ground sloping away like a shoreline. For one disorienting moment, Frank wasn't sitting in an unfinished boat in a suburban yard—he was already at sea, the vessel beneath him alive with purpose.

"I used to know what I was working on ... and why," Pastor Reed said. The words slipped out unbidden.

Franklin remained still, his profile etched against the deepening sky. No response. No acknowledgment.

"Frank, it looks like you're deep in it here. I'll ...

um ... leave you to it." Pastor Mike turned away, unsettled. The certainty he'd brought unraveled as he walked back to the car, leaving something raw and stripped bare.

He sank into the driver's seat and sat for a moment, hands resting on the wheel.

A sermon line he'd written that morning came to mind: "God moves in structure, in order, in the clear path of righteousness."

The words that had flowed so easily now felt brittle. Hollow.

Whatever Frank was doing, it had purpose. Mike couldn't name it, but he couldn't deny it.

And there, in the stillness of the car, the truth settled around him. The purpose that once lit his ministry had dimmed. The fire was still there—but now, it barely flickered.

* * *

Franklin stepped from the ladder to the deck, a small tin box tucked under his arm. The evening sky blazed deep red, then softened to purple.

On the deck, he paused and surveyed his work. A single nod. Quiet. Final.

Inside the box were three items: a charred button, a brass badge dulled with age, and a note, creased and faded.

With gentle care, he removed and unfolded the note. The handwriting was his wife's—slanted and sure.

"Keep building. Whatever it is, it will carry

more than you know."

Franklin read it once, then closed his eyes.

He pressed the note to the wooden railing for a moment, then placed it gently back in the box.

Inside the cabin, the small cupboard waited —its door carved with winding ivy, the latch polished smooth from his hands. He opened it, tucked the tin inside, and closed the door with a soft click.

Removing a polishing rag from his pocket, he gave the cupboard a final wipe, climbed down from the boat, extinguished the lantern, and went into the house.

* * *

The heavens opened at 2:00 am. The storm broke with a bright flash and immense peal of thunder; the voice of God rolling across the land. The strobe of lightning carried a green metallic cast, and was immediately chased by more crackling, booming thunder. Unlike a typical late summer shower, this resembled a spring boomer packed with torrential rain and the possibility of twisters. It seethed with energy.

Molly Carmichael sprang awake when the first crack of thunder split the air.

"It's starting." She'd scrambled for her flashlight, gel pens, and colored pencils to record everything in her diary.

June Lin rushed to her kitchen sink, woken early by nature's alarm clock. As the lightning flashed, she was amazed to see the old guy standing in the middle of it beside his boat, his face to the wind, eyes closed, as if listening for words in the storm. With each lightning flash, the wooden hull gleamed with an inner light that couldn't be explained by mere reflection. Something in his stillness amid the breaking storm made her breath catch.

From the sliding door leading to his deck Harlen looked out at Franklin's yard where the vessel loomed like a question he couldn't answer. In the rain cascading across the door's glass the boat seemed to rock slightly as if riding waves. A shiver ran through him that had nothing to do with the cold rain. "He really did it," Harlen whispered.

Pastor Reed jerked upright in bed, heart pounding. Rain lashed against the parsonage windows. Frank's weathered face filled his mind with unexpected clarity. The pastor felt a strange mixture of shame at his lack of understanding and awe at the persistence of the vision. Sliding from beneath the covers, he knelt beside his bed—not to offer words, but to listen to the storm.

Lightning forked across the sky, illuminating his sparse bedroom in harsh white light. In that frozen moment, the wall before him transformed. Where there should have been only the shadow of his dresser, he saw instead the silhouette of Franklin's boat—impossible, given the miles between them. In that flash, the boat became something more—something that called to the part of him that had grown silent, reminding him what sacred purpose once felt like.

The vision vanished with the darkness, but its impression remained. Mike lowered himself completely to the floor, hands outstretched and trembling slightly. For decades, he'd preached about sacred objects, holy places, divine purpose —all defined by words, by scripture, by careful interpretation.

Frank hadn't spoken a sentence; had offered no explanation.

The holiness that Pastor Reed had witnessed came not from declaration but from the simple act of creation. From purpose. From hands that built while others remained safe ... idle.

"I've had it backward."

He walked to his home office, switched on the light, gathered the sermon notes from his desk, and crushed them into a ball.

June listened as the rain pounded harder now, each drop a tiny percussive note against the window. She watched the guy standing immobile beside his creation, unfazed by the elements. Another flash of lightning illuminated the yard, and in that suspended moment, the boat's silhouette transformed.

Where she had seen only wood and nails before, now June saw an open book. The curved hull formed the spine, the cabin-like pages caught mid-turn by the wind. Something stirred within her—a recognition so sudden it made her gasp.

"My stories," she said out loud to the empty room.

For years abandoned for practicality, for steady work, for the business of continuing rather than creating. The vessel in Franklin's yard wasn't just his story—it was hers too, waiting to be written.

June remembered the shiver of gooseflesh when she knew—beyond doubt—that the sentence she'd just written was exactly right. She craved that again.

Harlen stood transfixed by the rain's relentless assault and the vision of the boat's tumultuous voyage on his patio door.

Lightning split the sky, bathing everything in stark, electric blue. In that frozen instant, the bow of the boat transformed. Where there had been only smooth curved planks and careful joinery, Harlen now saw an arched doorway—perfect, deliberate, and beckoning. Not a vessel meant for departure, but an entrance to something unnamed.

The vision lasted only a heartbeat, but it burned into his mind. This wasn't about sailing away. It was about stepping through.

Harlen uncurled his fingers from the door handle he hadn't realized he was gripping. For years he'd watched life pass, content to sit on porches, to joke and judge and wonder. Always on the outside looking in.

"A door," he murmured, understanding

blooming like heat in his chest. "Not a way out. A way in."

Outside Molly's window, the sky lit bright as day and the whole house seemed to vibrate. The sudden brilliance silhouetted Mr. Ames' creation against the night sky, transforming it. No longer just wooden planks—in that electric instant, the boat's sides spread outward like a great wing, poised for flight.

Molly pressed her nose against the cool glass, eyes wide. Her small hands splayed against the windowpane, leaving foggy prints that quickly faded. Another flash—and there it was again. Not a boat at all, but something becoming, stretching toward a shape it hadn't yet realized.

"It wants to fly."

She reached for her crayons without looking away from the window.

She would make something too. Something beautiful. Something ... becoming.

The rain stopped as suddenly as it had begun. Thunder that moments ago had shaken everything was gone, leaving behind an unsettling quiet, like the storm had delivered its message and was now waiting for a reply

* * *

Harlen held the cold beer bottle, condensation wetting his palm. The chair beneath him creaked —same sound it had made for fifteen years, faithful as an old dog. Across the fence, Franklin's boat caught the afternoon light.

Milton sat in the adjacent chair, knees cracking. "Your buddy's ark is still standing. I guess he knows a thing or two about building."

Harlen examined the structure rising above the fence line. The storm had left everything drenched —maple leaves still dripped, gutters gurgled— but he could picture the boat's planks, somehow untouched.

Milton took a long pull from his bottle, then waited, eyebrows raised slightly. The pause stretched between them where Harlen's usual joke should have been—something about Franklin's maritime delusions or retirement hobbies gone wild.

All he offered his friend was a grunt in reply.

Harlen lifted the bottle to his lips instead, tasting nothing. He looked at the surrounding houses in their familiar formation, lawns still puddled from the downpour.

The afternoon sun warmed his face. His thoughts circled the boat like birds around a lighthouse. Something about it nagged at him, pushed through the fog that had settled over his days. The words bubbled up before he could trap them.

"You ever feel like you've been waiting for something, but forgot what it was?"

Milton didn't answer. Just tilted his head, the movement barely visible in the gathering dusk.

Harlen leaned forward, elbows digging into his knees. "I wake up. Same coffee. Same game shows. Same Friday poker nights with the same jokes we've been telling since we had hair."

A chuckle escaped him, dry as autumn leaves. "All this time I thought I was settled. Turns out I was just parked."

Silence stretched between them. A breeze rustled the hedges, carrying the scent of wet earth and something sweeter—possibility, maybe.

"That man," Harlen continued, gesturing toward Franklin's yard with his bottle, "just started building like it mattered. Like something in him still needed making."

His voice softened, almost lost beneath the dripping eaves. "And I can't stop thinking about it. Like something under my ribs was stretching out. Wanting to move."

Milton pursed his lips as he studied Harlen. The quiet between them felt different than their usual comfortable silences—charged somehow, like the air before lightning strikes.

Harlen kept his gaze fixed on the blue horizon between the sun and the treetops. He wasn't looking for validation. The realization had settled into his bones with the certainty of gravity.

"It's not the boat," he said finally. "It's the doing. The why, not the what. The why not now?"

Harlen straightened in his chair, muscles tensing with unfamiliar purpose. He set his half-finished beer on the side table with a soft clink.

"Think I'll build something tomorrow."

Milton nodded slowly, thumb rubbing against his ring finger. "What?"

A smile—small but genuine—tugged at the corner of Harlen's mouth. "Don't know yet."

* * *

Molly's legs dangled over the edge of her bed as she hunched forward, diary pressed against her knees. The flashlight cast a wobbly circle of light on the page while shadows danced across her bedroom walls. She bit her tongue in concentration, pencil scratching across the paper.

September 1st. Dear Diary, TODAY was the BEST DAY!!! Mr. Ames let me in his boat!!!! Not just look at it but SIT IN IT!!!

Molly paused, tapping her pencil against her chin. She wanted to get the words exactly right.

He put his hands under my arms and lifted me up like I was light as a feather. His hands were all rough, but they were gentle. He put me right at the front part (the bow, he called it). I sat there with my legs crossed and it felt like it was floating even on the grass. Like magic.

She drew a quick sketch of herself sitting cross-legged at the front of the boat, hair flying behind her even though there wasn't any wind.

When I sat there I could see EVERYTHING different. Like I was already sailing. The trees looked like they were moving instead of me. I looked ahead like there was something coming, even though the boat doesn't move. Yet.

Molly squinted at her words, making sure she'd captured it right. That feeling when she'd sat in the captain's seat—like she was about to go somewhere important, somewhere nobody had ever been.

Molly added swirls around the boat in her drawing, making it look like it was surrounded by clouds or maybe magic. The thought made her pencil pause mid-stroke.

Mr. Ames never talks about where the boat will go. Mom asked him once and he just smiled. I think I know why now.

She pressed her pencil harder against the page, determined to get this important thought just right.

Maybe the boat's not for water. Maybe it's for hearts.

That sounded good. Grown-up, even. Like something her teacher might say was "profound." Molly wasn't entirely sure what that word meant, but she knew it was for big thoughts that made people stop and think.

The night pressed against her window. Stars peeked through the gap in her curtains, twinkling like they were trying to tell her something. Molly flipped to a fresh page and began a new drawing. This time, she sketched the boat hovering above the rooftops of Bramble Hollow Drive. Instead of clouds or sky beneath it, she carefully drew stars— dozens of them, some big, some small, all shining up instead of down.

Her pencil moved with certainty now. The boat didn't look silly floating above the houses. It looked right, like that's where it belonged all along.

At the bottom of the page, she wrote in her neatest handwriting: *Mr. Ames didn't build it to go somewhere. He built it so we'd remember we still can.*

Molly smiled at her work, satisfied. That was it exactly.

Afterward

I would like to extend a sincere thank you for spending time with these stories. I hope you enjoyed reading them as much as I enjoyed creating them—probably not, but I can hope. I also hope that something has spoken to you in a memorable and meaningful way, and that our lives and world are slightly better because our paths crossed here.

Below is a link to access the book information and leave a review. I would be extremely grateful for any feedback you would be kind enough to provide. Thank you!

Link to Book Details

Scan to View on Amazon

Discussion Guide

The Measure of More was written to spark both introspection and enjoyment. If you're reading this collection with a book club or small group, the following questions are designed to foster meaningful conversation and deeper reflection on the themes woven through each story and the collection as a whole.

To guide your discussion, you'll find:
- A set of collection-wide questions for exploring overarching themes.
- A Top 5 list of key questions for each story—ideal for discussing the entire collection in a single session.
- A Going Deeper section for each story, offering additional prompts for more focused or extended conversation.

COLLECTION-WIDE DISCUSSION QUESTIONS

1. Each story explores a different kind of "more"— achievement, approval, security, expertise, comfort. Which story's version of "more" felt most familiar to you, and why?

2. Across the collection, characters are asked to choose between external validation and internal authenticity. How did different characters respond to that tension—and where do you find yourself in that spectrum?

3. Several stories include literal or symbolic notebooks, diaries, or margin notes. How does the act of writing—whether in secret, in public, or in reflection—serve as a tool for transformation?

4. From Marcy's potluck to Diego's communal cooking to Franklin's boat-building, shared spaces and simple acts often become catalysts for connection. What small, everyday moments have helped you rediscover purpose or belonging?

5. Many characters initially define themselves by their roles—chef, photographer, HOA enforcer, preacher—but later reclaim a deeper identity. What does the collection suggest about who we

are beyond our titles or achievements?

6. Spiritual depth and faith emerge in subtle, often messy ways—not always in churches or through formal rituals. Which story most expanded your view of what spiritual growth can look like?

7. If you were to write a new story for this collection—based on your own life or someone you know—what kind of "more" would be at the center of the tension?

8. After reading The Measure of More, what "more" are you being invited to release—and what might you be called to embrace instead?

THE NOTE SHE HELD - TOP 5

1. How does Callie's tension between singing for applause and singing from the heart reflect the broader struggle between external recognition and inner authenticity?

2. Callie's mother pushes her toward visibility and validation. In what ways does this reflect cultural or societal pressure to perform—and how does that clash with Callie's personal values?

3. Compare Callie's relationships with her mother and her grandfather. How does each influence her evolving sense of success, identity, and purpose?

4. Though this story focuses on music, the tension between "status" and "authenticity" appears in many areas of life—careers, parenting, social media. Choose one and discuss how you navigate it personally.

5. Have you ever felt pressured to pursue a path that didn't reflect your true self? How did you respond—and what would you do differently, knowing what you know now?

THE NOTE SHE HELD - GOING DEEPER

6. The congregation's silence after Callie's solo carries unexpected weight. Why might that silence speak more powerfully than applause—

and how does it affirm the story's theme of authenticity?

7. From being volunteered for the solo to claiming the moment as her own, what key turning points shape Callie's emotional transformation?

8. What does Callie's mother's pushiness reveal about her own unfulfilled aspirations? Where does her desire to support become entangled with her need for validation?

9. Grandpa Walter supports Callie through quiet presence rather than pressure. How does his influence help her rediscover her voice—and what does that contrast teach us?

10. Callie's friends want to share her performance online. How do their well-meaning reactions reflect today's tension between public recognition and private meaning?

11. The story's physical settings shift—from the sanctuary to the kitchen to Grandpa's room. How do these spaces mirror the emotional atmosphere and Callie's inner journey?

12. Why does singing the Easter hymn her way serve as the emotional climax of the story? What narrative threads build to make that moment feel earned and resonant?

13. By adjusting the tempo and dynamics of the hymn, Callie makes an intentional artistic choice. How does this become an act of resistance—and why is that moment crucial to the theme of self-expression?

14. Callie realizes that "truth has a different resonance" and doesn't need to shout. How can we apply this idea in our own lives, especially in a world obsessed with volume and visibility?

15. Encouragement can easily slip into projection. How can we better support others in finding their own path—especially children or loved ones—without overshadowing their individuality?

SEASONED WITH WISDOM - TOP 5

1. How does the tension between Diego's "culinary art" and Esther's simple comfort food reflect the broader conflict between creating for recognition and creating to meet real human needs?

2. Diego's technical brilliance initially isolates him. How does the story explore the difference between knowledge used to impress and wisdom used to connect?

3. Esther's "Comfort Food Social" fosters genuine community. What does the story suggest about the kind of wisdom that goes beyond skill to cultivate shared experience?

4. Compare the leadership styles of Diego (precise, authoritative) and Esther (gentle, collaborative). How do their approaches shape their relationships with the residents—and eventually, with each other?

5. Seasoned with Wisdom thrives on shared stories and simple meals. What's one small, intentional way you could use food, storytelling, or another shared experience to build connection this week?

SEASONED WITH WISDOM - GOING DEEPER

6. Diego's obsession with perfect plating and food photography reveals a desire for external

validation. How does the story contrast that with a deeper, quieter form of wisdom rooted in service?

7. Esther's cafeteria experience is about nourishment and connection. How do her motivations highlight the gap between feeding for care versus performing for prestige?

8. Diego's pride clashes with the residents' needs in moments like the failed training and overly fancy dishes. How do these moments move him—gradually—from performance toward humility?

9. Each resident brings a specific memory of food —lake trout, casseroles, apple cake. How do these stories act as a form of lived culinary wisdom, reshaping Diego's understanding of what matters?

10. The story moves from Diego's solitary prep station to a lively communal kitchen. How does this change in setting reflect the internal transformation from ego to collaboration?

11. The "Vending Machine Communion" scene offers quiet but sharp critique. How does it foreshadow Esther's Comfort Food Social—and deepen the story's commentary on where true nourishment comes from?

12. When Diego sets aside his tweezers and joins the group, it's a small gesture with big meaning. What does this act symbolize in terms of identity, humility, and the shift from perfection to presence?

13. Have you ever devoted time to developing a skill mainly for recognition? What would it look like to redirect that effort toward service or shared meaning instead?

14. Esther values folk wisdom—recipes passed down, hands-on know-how. In your own life, is there someone whose practical knowledge you've undervalued? How might you learn from them?

15. Technical excellence can impress, but without empathy it often rings hollow. How do you personally evaluate whether your skills are serving others—or simply feeding your ego?

BLESSED ARE THE WEARY - TOP 5

1. At the beginning of the story, Dana senses gossip and judgment within the congregation. How does her internal dialogue contrast with the outward behaviors around her—and what does this tension suggest about the difference between appearance and belonging?
2. Dana remains active in church life while grieving deeply. How does the story explore the gap between participation in ritual and the experience of inner pain?
3. Compare Dana's perception of "church people" to Barbara Nolan's quiet, personal outreach. What does the story imply about the difference between performing grace and truly embodying it?
4. Sam paints rotting fruit, and Barbara affirms its emotional truth. How does this "raw and honest" art offer a deeper expression of faith than conventional religious behavior?
5. Have you ever found yourself going through religious or social motions while feeling unseen or unsupported? What might it look like to offer or receive empathy that moves beyond ritual?

BLESSED ARE THE WEARY - GOING DEEPER

6. Pastor Reed's sermon draws from 1 Corinthians 15:58. How does that verse resonate—or fall flat—for Dana in the midst of her grief? What does the story suggest about when and how scripture offers real comfort?

7. Cheryl's encouragements—"You will rise," "Blessed are the Strong"—are well-meant, but often feel hollow. How does Dana's reaction reveal the limits of spiritual platitudes during deep suffering?

8. Dana throws herself into volunteering, cleaning, and staying busy. How do these coping strategies offer short-term protection, yet also prevent her from receiving the support she truly needs?

9. Though Cheryl genuinely cares, her default is to offer activity over empathy. How does this highlight the difference between trying to fix grief and being willing to sit with it?

10. Barbara listens, shares her own story, and invites Dana into creative expression. How does her approach embody grace—and why does it carry more healing power than advice or distraction?

11. Sam's decaying fruit paintings are emotionally raw, while Dana clings to composure. What does their contrast reveal about generational differences in expressing faith, grief, and emotional honesty?

12. Why might Dana's private expression of anger while throwing out Ron's things feel

more honest than her public participation in ministry? What does this say about the gap between her internal reality and external expectations?

13. The community center's sterile lighting and makeshift dividers contrast with Barbara's warmth. How does the setting itself reflect the story's tension between institutional religion and unpolished grace?

14. Barbara says, "I've walked in your shoes," and responds with empathy instead of performance. Who in your own life might need that kind of unguarded, experience-shaped presence?

15. Have you ever felt pressure to hide your pain in a community of faith or friendship? What would it take to build a space—like Barbara's art room—where people feel safe enough to be fully seen?

MARCY'S NOTEBOOK AND THE
CANINE CONSPIRACY - TOP 5

1. How does the neighborhood's strict uniformity —identical lawns, roofs, and holiday décor rules—create emotional distance between residents? What begins to shift when that façade is disrupted?
2. Marcy believes she's protecting the neighborhood by enforcing rules, yet remains isolated. How does the story reveal the unintended consequences of control disguised as care?
3. Marcy begins alone, documenting infractions. By the end, the neighborhood is hosting potlucks and book clubs. How does the story contrast solitary missions with shared purpose in building community?
4. Murphy's unpredictable "gifts" push neighbors to connect. Have you ever experienced a small disruption or surprise that unexpectedly brought people together? What changed as a result?
5. Think of a personal habit or mindset—like Marcy's rule enforcement—that might keep you emotionally guarded. What's one small, intentional change you could make to foster connection instead?

MARCY'S NOTEBOOK AND THE CANINE
CONSPIRACY - GOING DEEPER

6. Marcy's morning ritual and detailed note-taking bring her comfort—but also reinforce her distance from others. How can personal routines both shelter and isolate us?

7. Marcy's Community Log starts as a tool for control but eventually helps foster connection. What key moments shift her understanding of how her skills can serve rather than separate?

8. Murphy's habit of stealing slippers, tennis balls, and other objects draws neighbors into reluctant interaction. How does this nonverbal chaos become a surprising bridge across social divides?

9. Claire's sarcasm and Jeremy's lighthearted schemes challenge Marcy's assumptions. How do their responses to Murphy model playful connection and nudge her toward change?

10. Marcy's memories of Ben shape her initial isolation—but also become a quiet catalyst for reconnection. When does remembering shift from retreating inward to reaching outward?

11. Murphy's wandering and object collection feel random—but they seem to reflect what's missing in people's lives. How does he symbolically restore forgotten or overlooked connections?

12. Marcy's notebook begins as a record of neighborhood violations, but transforms into a log of community activities. How does its changing purpose mirror her emotional transformation?

13. The HOA meeting's formal structure stands in contrast to the casual potluck planning. How does this shift in tone reflect the story's theme of moving from performance to participation?

14. Have you ever prioritized rules, routines, or high standards over connection—and ended up feeling lonely? What's one way you could introduce more flexibility into your daily life to make space for people?

15. Marcy eventually uses her love of order to coordinate book clubs and potlucks. What's one small way you could use your strengths to spark community in your own neighborhood or social circle?

THREE MINUTES TO SUNSET - TOP 5

1. Marcus hopes the $25k prize will solve his family's financial strain. How does this urgency shape his decisions—and how does the story explore the way busyness can feel necessary, even noble?

2. What does Marcus risk—and almost lose—in his pursuit of the perfect shot, and what does this reveal about how we define success in high-pressure seasons of life?

3. The contest offers professional prestige and "National Geographic" exposure. How does the story challenge the assumption that success in one area of life guarantees fulfillment in another?

4. Marcus repeatedly tells Sarah, "just five more minutes," while chasing a future that may never arrive. What does this reveal about the emotional cost of postponing presence for productivity?

5. Think of a moment you nearly missed—or did miss—because your attention was elsewhere. What practice or mindset shift might help you stay grounded in what matters most next time?

THREE MINUTES TO SUNSET - GOING DEEPER

6. The story contrasts the elusive "green flash"

with Harper's very real first steps. What does this juxtaposition say about the difference between capturing a perfect moment and truly experiencing one?

7. Marcus frequently promises "just a few more minutes," but fails to follow through. How does this repeated delay shape his relationship with Sarah—and what does it say about the erosion of trust through small dismissals?

8. From missed calls to obsessing over camera settings, Marcus overlooks signs of strain at home. How do these blind spots reveal how ambition can mask emotional unavailability?

9. Sarah's decision to show up at the quarry marks a turning point. What does her action convey about the unseen labor of caregiving and the emotional toll of Marcus's absence?

10. The XF200 lens represents Marcus's dream— but also its weight. How does this piece of equipment symbolize both his aspirations and the burdens his pursuit places on his family?

11. The story's recurring timestamps—"three minutes to sunset," "five days to deadline"— intensify the narrative pressure. How do they mirror Marcus's inner sense of urgency and fear of falling short?

12. The contrast between the cramped home (with bills and baby gear) and the vast quarry overlook reflects Marcus's divided priorities. How do these two settings externalize his internal conflict?

13. Sarah shows love by showing up, while Marcus envisions love through providing or achieving. How do these contrasting expressions of care highlight the story's theme of presence over performance?
14. Marcus meticulously plans every aspect of the quarry shoot—but is blindsided by Harper's milestone. How does his desire to control outcomes blind him to the most meaningful, uncontrollable moments of life?
15. Can you recall a time when chasing a goal led you to miss something irreplaceable? What habit or boundary might you adopt to remain present with the people who matter most?

MARGIN NOTES - TOP 5

1. Ren often turns to distractions—TV, phone, casual hookups—as a way to avoid deeper reflection. How does this avoidance mirror our own tendencies to escape rather than confront life's harder questions?

2. The contrast between the printed line "The soul seeks shape" and the handwritten note "Let it stay messy" highlights the tension between rigid doctrine and lived experience. How does that tension shape the story's core message?

3. Ren's gender is never explicitly revealed. Did you imagine Ren as male or female? What influenced that assumption, and what might it reveal about your own subconscious expectations or biases?

4. In the coffee shop, Ren moves between surface-level "busywork" and a moment of true presence with Anna. What do these two types of engagement suggest about the difference between distraction and spiritual vulnerability?

5. The note "Let it stay messy" implies that growth often comes through embracing imperfection. What part of your life feels most uncertain or unresolved right now—and how might you lean into that messiness with honesty and grace?

MARGIN NOTES - GOING DEEPER

6. Ren's decision to straighten a crooked poster and help a stranger at Panda Market may seem small, but they mark internal shifts. What do these subtle actions suggest about moving from distraction toward spiritual awareness?

7. The handwritten notes in Roots of Being offer personal reflections that contrast with the book's formal tone. How do these margin notes symbolize a spiritual life that values honesty over certainty?

8. Ren admits to being "checked out since about 2018." How does this self-awareness signal spiritual stagnation—and what signs of growth emerge as the story unfolds?

9. Anna's cheerful demeanor masks her grief, just as Ren's distractions mask their emptiness. How does their moment of vulnerability with each other highlight the role of honest connection in deepening spiritual life?

10. The anonymous notes from June Lin spark something in Ren. How does this unseen character serve as a kind of spiritual companion—and what does that say about the power of shared wisdom across time?

11. The story hints at past abandonment, but Ren's detachment seems rooted in multiple habits of avoidance. What experiences in the story suggest a shift to confront—or reshape—those

habits?

12. Helping a stranger without hesitation marks a turning point for Ren. How does this act of empathy contrast with earlier behaviors—and what does it reveal about the healing nature of unguarded kindness?

13. Roots of Being was once discarded, then found, then returned. How does the journey of this book reflect Ren's own movement from spiritual neglect toward tentative re-engagement?

14. Ren's early-morning walk without headphones is a quiet moment of change. How does choosing ambient sound over constant stimulation reflect a willingness to be present with life as it is?

15. What habitual distractions—social media, entertainment, busyness—might you be using to avoid deeper questions? What small shift could help you cultivate presence and authenticity in your own life?

THE ARK ON BRAMBLE HOLLOW DRIVE - TOP 5

1. Franklin's yard is an unlikely place for a boat. How does the story suggest that meaningful purpose often emerges in unexpected environments, not within the safety of the familiar?
2. Several neighbors spend days simply watching Franklin. How does the story contrast passive observation with the harder, more personal work of discovering one's own calling?
3. Many characters first glimpse the boat across a boundary—Molly from her blanket fort, Harlen from his porch, June from her kitchen window. How do these physical barriers reflect the emotional and spiritual hesitation to step beyond comfort zones?
4. Harlen describes his routine as "parked" living. What does Franklin's quiet, determined labor teach about the link between uncertainty and purposeful movement?
5. The boat's power seems to lie more in the act of building than in any finished result. Is there a project, habit, or dream you've left dormant that could be revived—without needing it to be perfect or complete right away?

THE ARK ON BRAMBLE HOLLOW
DRIVE - GOING DEEPER

6. Pastor Mike arrives with scripture, but is moved more deeply by Franklin's silent devotion. How does the story explore spiritual depth as something communicated more powerfully through presence than through prepared words?

7. Molly says the boat is for "carrying feelings." How does her childlike wonder and imagination challenge the adults' skepticism—and what does this suggest about the nature of purpose and faith?

8. In what ways does Molly use imagination in her diary to make sense of Franklin's boat? What does this tell us about how children use stories and images to understand their world?

9. Harlen moves from mocking Franklin to envying his purpose. How does his shift reveal the tension between comfort in routine and a buried longing for deeper meaning?

10. June watches Franklin and recalls her unfinished novel. How does witnessing his steady work prompt her to reevaluate her own creative purpose—and what does this say about reclaiming abandoned dreams?

11. Franklin's boat is never launched, yet it impacts everyone who sees it. How does its incomplete or unrealized state symbolize that purpose isn't always about finishing—but about ongoing faithfulness to the task?

12. Franklin's backstory as a firefighter and his wife's encouragement to "keep building"

suggest a personal source for his calling. How do loss and memory shape someone's sense of purpose—even when it seems impractical or misunderstood?

13. The storm reveals the boat in a different form to each character. How does this shared moment serve as a personal awakening for each of them—and what does it suggest about the individualized nature of calling?

14. Written reflections—like Molly's diary and June's book margins—quietly contrast with the louder voices of doubt. How do these introspective acts reveal the value of private reflection in uncovering meaning?

15. Franklin never explains his purpose, yet his steady actions inspire transformation. What would it look like to commit to a quiet act of creativity or service in your own life—not for recognition, but because it matters?